An

by Heather Gray

an Informal Romance novella

in celebration of my Savior
in memory of my daughter
with pride in my son
with gratitude for my husband

But as it is, God arranged the members in the body,
each one of them, as he chose.
1 Corinthians 12:18

One

Here he comes again.

Kimi pretended to organize her muffin assortment as Dr. No-Name approached. She could set her clock by him. Every Monday, Wednesday, and Friday at 7:05 in the morning, he came for his large half-caff triple nonfat medium whip white mocha. Even though she knew what he would order, she waited for him to arrive. One day not too long ago, she'd started his drink as soon as he'd stepped into view. She'd had the steaming beverage ready and waiting for him. The poor guy had been so flustered he'd knocked over the fruit basket and taken out half the cookie display in the process.

She'd learned an important lesson that day. Two, really. Patience paid off. And some people don't handle change well.

Dr. No-Name glanced to the side and tripped over a covered cable that ran along the floor. He kicked the toe of his loafer into the top of the cable's molded rubber protector, lost his balance, hopped a couple of times on his left foot, swung his arms like a grade-schooler doing the windmill in PE, and finally got his right shoe back down on the ground. Despite the theatrical gymnastics, nobody but her appeared to be watching the show. She had to give him points for the landing. Not a brown hair on his head was out of place, and his lab coat hung from his shoulders with straight lines in complete denial of its recent whirlwind of activity.

The same cable had been positioned across that floor for as long as Kimi could remember. The doctor had to know it, too, but unless his eyes were trained directly on it, he seemed to forget. She'd witnessed his footwork often enough to realize that much, at least.

Kimi turned her back on him lest he catch her spying. Despite his oddities, she enjoyed Dr. No-Name's visits to her kiosk and didn't want to scare him off by staring or — heaven forbid — laughing.

"Um, excuse me."

She turned around, her smile in place and hopefully no pity in her eyes. "Good morning! The usual?"

Dr. No-Name nodded. Most doctors wore their name embroidered on their official white lab coats, but not this one. Plain white, no fancy frills, and no embroidery. Either he wasn't important enough for a name on his coat or he was humble enough not to care. She secretly hoped it was the latter.

Kimi set to work on his drink and tried to make conversation. "You always order a triple shot, but you want half-caff. Most people who want to go easy on the caffeine avoid the triple."

She caught his shrug out of the corner of her eye. Getting this guy to talk was harder than pulling a barking dog's molars with a pair of tweezers.

"There must be a reason. What about the triple shot do you find inviting?"

He blinked a couple of times, masking the bright blue of his eyes, before answering. "I like the taste of the triple, but I don't want a caffeine high."

She'd figured as much. As a coffee aficionado, she could understand. She loved the flavor but wasn't always interested in the calories or the caffeine. Like him, she'd learned to improvise.

She handed over his drink, and Dr. No-Name passed her three ones, two quarters, one dime, and one nickel. That was the other reason he remained a no-name. Had he ever paid with credit card, she would know his name by now. He always paid in cash, though. The exact $3.65 including tax.

"There's going to be a price increase later this month. I don't know the date yet or the new prices, but I thought I should warn you."

His turn away from her kiosk stalled. "Why?"

"Why am I warning you, or why the change?"

He reached for a napkin and wiped off the spotless customer side of the counter. "Why the increase?"

It was her turn to shrug. "The late summer rains have been too heavy. Flooding ruined a good part of South America's coffee crop. Our owner expects to see an exponential hike in bean prices over the coming year, so he's trying to get ahead of things with a small increase now. He hopes doing that will allow him to postpone a larger increase."

"Supply and demand." He was a master at being succinct.

"Pretty much. Kind of the same reason why some pharmaceutical drugs are so expensive."

He shook his head. "That's an erroneous comparison. Coffee crops depend on nature to thrive. Pharmaceuticals are almost all manmade these days. If a company wants the price of their drug to go up, they can choose to make less of it. Decisions like that happen in boardrooms. Nobody chose to ruin their coffee crop."

Kimi wiped the imaginary crumbs off the small counter near her cash register. "Excellent point. Do you think pharmaceutical companies actually do that? Make less so they can charge more?"

A shadow passed over his face, transforming his normally blue eyes into an obscure shade of grey. "Some do. It's a fact of doing business. There are others, though, that I think... I hope... maintain integrity." With a brisk nod in her direction, he turned and headed back the way he'd come. He stopped before he came to the site of his previous trip. Kimi would have loved to see the look on his face as he took a higher-than-usual step over the rubberized cable protector.

Dr. No-Name fascinated her, but she still hadn't figured out why. She didn't get many doctors in her part of the hospital. Near the surgical waiting room, her kiosk put her in a position to deal almost exclusively with family members. Doctors didn't usually come this way — at least not for coffee. What's more, Dr. No-Name always approached from her right, which meant he came from within the hospital, not from the parking garage. There had to be other kiosks more convenient to his location than hers.

Oh well. She'd gotten him to talk more today than any day previous. Maybe he'd still be talkative come Friday. If so, she might even be able to pull a name out of him.

All for the sake of making conversation and putting her customers at ease, of course.

TWO

Owen rounded the corner and leaned against the wall. He took a sip and glanced back toward the coffee kiosk. The edge came into view, enough for him to catch movement, but not enough for him to get a good look at Kimi.

Just as well. He never knew what to say to her. The petite pixie with brown hair and eyes had tried to chat with him nearly every time he'd purchased coffee from her, but conversation wasn't easy for him. The fact that she hadn't given up on him yet was no small miracle. She would eventually. Common sense said so. His stomach clenched at the thought. Despite the way he always found himself at a loss for words when around her, he regularly bypassed three other kiosks to get to hers whenever he spent his day on-site at the hospital.

Owen shook his head and pushed off from the wall. With any luck, he'd make it back to his office without tripping or spilling coffee on his newly cleaned lab coat. Some doctors managed to wear the same coat for an entire week. Not him. His dry cleaner, a petite woman with an accent placing ancestry somewhere south of Russia and north of Australia, beamed with glee every time she caught sight of him at her counter. He couldn't blame her. After all, he was single-handedly putting her grandchildren through college.

Knee-deep in spreadsheets, Owen answered, "Go away," when someone knocked on his office door. He needed to analyze the latest data set and couldn't be bothered with people. Didn't anybody understand how important his work was?

The knock came again, this time louder. On the tip of his tongue, the words, "Leave me alone," begged to be spoken, but he bit them back. Even if he didn't always act like it, he believed people mattered. He cared about them. He just... didn't like to be interrupted.

His sigh echoed in the room as Owen pushed himself back from his desk and moved stiffly to the door. How long had he been sitting anyway? A quick glance at his watch told him. Four hours. He'd been pouring over data for four hours without moving. Regardless of who was on the other side of the door, he should welcome the interruption.

Owen pulled the door open and admitted Dr. Jameson.

The older man entered with the familiarity of someone not the least-bit put out by the previous order to *go away.* "Have you looked over the latest data set yet?"

Owen nodded. "I've been reading through it for the last four hours."

"It looked promising at first glance. Does it bear up under further scrutiny?" Dr. Jameson retrieved a bottle of water from the small fridge Owen kept in his office. Then he sank into the olive drab couch pushed up against one wall.

"Yes." Without much choice in the matter, Owen lowered himself onto the uncomfortable wooden chair opposite the couch. He never should have admitted to Dr. Jameson that he'd gotten the ergonomically atrocious chair so people would leave sooner whenever they came to speak to him. His mentor had been happily settling into the comfortable couch ever since.

"The board wants to see the drug released within six months. Is that feasible?"

Owen closed his eyes and counted to twenty.

Dr. Jameson had been his professor in a microcellular pharmacology class he'd taken in med school. He was also the man Owen had turned to when, upon completion of his residency, his lack of people skills had forced him to rethink a career in pediatric oncology. Dr. Jameson was the one who had listened to him talk for hours about a drug concept he'd developed in his limited spare time. He could go on. He owed the man on his couch. Even more so because Dr. Jameson understood him and wasn't put off by his oddities.

Another internal count to twenty and a deep breath later, Owen answered. "I want to tell you no, because I think more testing should be done. We haven't solved the blood sugar problem yet. As long as it's monitored, though..." He shrugged. "We've followed all the proper protocols, and so technically, yes, the drug will be ready to release in six months." Despite the throbbing in his temple every time the subject was brought up, Owen added, "It can be released as soon as the FDA approves it."

Dr. Jameson took a long draw on his bottle of water. "How many deaths has the blood sugar issue caused?"

"Two. We then adjusted our protocol to require daily testing."

"For the duration of treatment?"

Owen shook his head. Dr. Jameson knew the answer, so why ask? "The data has shown that patients who have no extreme fluctuations in their blood sugar during the first four months won't develop them at all, so we only make them test for the first four months. If we see spikes and drops during that period, then we keep them testing longer and supplement our drug with whatever is necessary to stabilize their blood sugar. We can't say, though, whether or not those additional medications will interfere with the effectiveness of our treatment. It'll take months before we know that for sure."

Dr. Jameson tapped his left hand absently against his knee. "We can include that in our warning label. Explain we don't yet know the efficacy of continuing the drug in patients whose blood sugars fluctuate under treatment."

Owen gave a mechanical nod. "I still don't understand. It's a cancer drug, and nothing in this drug should affect the pancreas. Where is this reaction coming from?"

"What percent of trial participants experience the blood sugar side effect?"

"Fewer than ten percent of patients."

"And only two deaths?"

Owen followed Dr. Jameson's lead. "Yes, and if we'd required blood sugar testing rather than suggesting it at that stage, those two would still be alive. So we updated the protocol to move it from a suggestion to a requirement. We make the parents sign paperwork where they agree to administer a daily blood glucose check on their child."

Dr. Jameson nodded. "When you say the drug needs more testing, are you referring to anything besides the blood sugar? Do you harbor any other concerns that we haven't already addressed?"

Owen shook his head. They'd covered everything. He could continue to look for the cause of the blood sugar problem even after the drug released.

"Good. There's something else I need to talk to you about."

The change in Dr. Jameson's voice gave warning. Whatever was coming next, Owen wouldn't like it.

"Do you remember when I explained why we wanted to relocate you from Chicago to our lab here in Virginia?"

Owen remembered all right. He'd hoped, however, that the pharmaceutical company would wise up and realize they were better off not forcing the issue.

"It's time." Dr. Jameson built a funeral pyre with his voice.

Owen's stomach dropped despite the uncomfortably angled chair that seemed to want to force all his internal organs northward.

"Gyermeck Pharmaceuticals will be asking the FDA to fast-track the drug. All our paperwork is in order, and our stats back up the drug's release. The waiting period with the FDA, though, is... problematic."

"A Pomeranian has more chance of convincing a government agency to take action. You send me in there, and the drug will end up permanently sidelined." Owen knew his limitations. People were one of his biggest.

Dr. Jameson's mouth lifted at the corner. "I'm not asking you to go into a meeting or address Congress. Nothing of the sort."

Owen should feel better, but he would reserve judgment until Dr. Jameson finished. "Then what?"

"There's a reception..."

"Uh-uh. No way. Seriously? A social gathering? I'd rather testify before Congress if it's all the same to you."

"Unfortunately, it's not all the same, and Gyermeck isn't backing down on this. The reception is next Thursday night. That gives you eight days to procure a tux and a date. Find someone who can fill in the awkward silences for you. If you don't..."

Owen was still shaking his head. "Sending me to a social gathering like that will guarantee Gyermeck never gets approval to release the drug."

Dr. Jameson stood and moved toward the door. "I know it's not what you wanted to hear, but it's part of your contract. I'll check back with you on Tuesday to make sure you have a tuxedo and a date."

"And if I don't?"

"I've been instructed to see to it that you attend even if it means I dress you myself and hire an escort to accompany you."

The door closed behind Dr. Jameson, but Owen remained in the chair. He was supposed to find a date to take to a reception — presumably a government reception — or the pharmaceutical company financing his research would hire one for him.

Could the day get any worse?

A crack echoed in the confined space of his office.

Oh no...

Owen landed on the floor.

Time for a new chair.

Three

Kimi hurried into the sanctuary and settled into the back pew with as little fuss as she could manage. She normally attended church on Saturday evening because she worked on Sundays, but a young friend was slotted to sing a solo today, and she'd promised to be there for the performance. Kimi had needed to do a bit of wheedling, but she'd even talked her brother into covering part of her shift at the hospital so she could make it.

Not more than thirty seconds after her backside hit the cushioned pew, Makayla's voice filled the sanctuary. The lilting chords of "Blessings" wrapped around Kimi's heart and squeezed.

Makayla had just turned thirteen the first time they'd met at a church picnic. Kimi hadn't known what to make of the young girl with a beautiful smile and bald head. Then her brother's wife had leaned close and whispered, "Cancer," and Kimi had been lost.

Getting acquainted with Makayla had kept her in Virginia. She'd only planned on visiting before returning to her happily bohemian life in Portland, Oregon. Kimi had mentioned her artwork in passing, though, and Makayla had latched on, telling her all about the art programs at the hospital and how desperately the kids needed trained art therapists.

Art had always been the secret to Kimi's peace. Her art was where she and God most often met, how they talked to each other. God was a part of her life every day, all day. He spoke to her more intimately, though, when she was in the midst of creating. And in its own way, art healed. Kimi had known that. Before Makayla, though, she hadn't realized that other people understood, too — that schools taught people how to use art to treat and heal those who bore invisible wounds deep inside their soul.

Ultimately, Kimi applied to Washington University and had been inching her way toward her Master's in Art Therapy ever since.

Makayla's voice reached the crescendo before dropping to the whisper soft ending of the song as chills raced up and down Kimi's spine. That girl had suffered more than most in her short life. Yet she stood in front of all those people and sang to them about God's blessings coming through the difficulties and trials of life. Some people struggled with finding hope on the brightest days, but Makayla grabbed onto it with both hands on the darkest days, too. She set an example for everyone, Kimi included.

Church let out, and Kimi rose from her seat. Mr. Maskey, Makayla's dad, was in her sights. She knew the teen couldn't be far behind him, so she pursued him. Working against the crowd the way she was, though, he soon slipped away in all the bustle. Kimi gave up the battle and climbed up on a pew and looked out across the sanctuary. She was five feet tall in her heels, but she'd left the heels at home. She couldn't even aspire to five feet in her tennis shoes. Up on the pew, though, she might have a chance...

Once she spotted Mr. Maskey again, she jumped down, bumped into someone who frowned at her, and made her way in the right direction. They were going to lunch together, but she was supposed to be back at her coffee kiosk by two o'clock. They needed to hurry if she hoped to return on time.

The crowd began to thin out as Kimi continued to push her way toward the front of the sanctuary where she'd last spotted her quarry. As she broke past the last human barrier, she swiped a hand through her cropped hair. "Man! This church needs a mosh pit. Then they could've bodysurfed me up here. I guarantee I'd have gotten fewer elbows to the sternum that way."

"We're so glad you could make it." Mrs. Maskey's voice welcomed her.

Kimi threw her a smile. "Wouldn't have missed it. Makayla did a beautiful job."

"We think so, too, but then, we're biased." Mrs. Maskey's eyes twinkled in the soft lighting. "Are you ready for lunch? I know you're on a schedule, so we were just going across the street to the deli."

"Sounds perfect. Where's Makayla, though? I didn't see her."

Mrs. Maskey pointed over Kimi's right shoulder. "She's talking to Dr. Pratt."

Dr. Pratt? The brilliant — and *hot* according to the teen — doctor who had reinvented the treatment for Makayla's particular type of cancer? The Maskeys spoke of him often enough that Kimi felt like she knew him personally. Meeting him would be a delight.

She turned, eager to get a glimpse of the marvelous Dr. Pratt.

And her jaw dropped.

When the doctor noticed her staring, his eyebrows drew together. "You stood on a pew."

He was the one who'd frowned at her when she'd gotten down from the pew, too. Only, she hadn't recognized him without his white lab coat on. "*You're* Dr. Pratt?"

The Dr. No-Name she'd been serving coffee to for the past several months was none other than the vaunted Dr. Pratt, future winner of the Nobel Prize in Medicine if the Maskeys could be believed.

"Do you make a habit of standing on other people's furniture?"

Kimi shook her head to clear the fog. "What?"

Dr. Pratt's frown remained in place. "You stood on a pew. Do you stand on the furniture when you go to someone else's house?"

Oh dear. He wasn't going to lecture her about this being God's house, was he? She already knew that. "I lost sight of Mr. Maskey. I wanted to locate him again."

Makayla looped her arm through Kimi's. "Is everyone ready for lunch? It's okay if Dr. Pratt joins us, right Mom? I invited him."

Mrs. Maskey glanced from Kimi to the doctor. "Of course, dear. The more the merrier, right?"

Makayla led the way, Kimi in tow, as they walked out into the bright sunlight.

Dr. Pratt's disapproval followed them.

"So what'd you order, Dr. P?" Thank goodness Makayla was able to make conversation. Kimi was at a loss, and neither Mr. nor Mrs. Maskey seemed inclined to fill the awkward silence.

"Italian beef. You?"

"I like the plain ol' turkey club. What's on the Italian beef?"

Dr. Pratt, the man who until recently couldn't be bothered to string more than two words together when speaking to Kimi, answered Makayla at length. "It's a Chicago classic. Slow-cooked beef served on a hoagie roll with peppers and then dipped in its own *jus.*"

"Um..." Makayla wrinkled her nose. "So, kind of like a French dip?"

Dr. Pratt laughed. Out loud. Kimi hadn't heard his laugh before, but she liked it. It was warm and carefree, so at odds with the man himself.

"You did hear me say Italian beef, right? Nothing French about it."

Makayla rolled her eyes. "What makes it so special then that calling it French is an insult?"

The doctor watched the waitress as she approached with their orders. "It's tradition. You can't grow up anywhere near Chicago without learning to love Italian beef. It's practically a rite of passage."

Mr. Maskey opened his bag of chips and set it aside. "Does that mean the deli's owner is from Chicago?"

Dr. Pratt tipped his head toward the counter. "He says so, but I won't know for sure till I take a bite."

"Come on, everyone. Let's say the blessing. Would you like to pray, Dr. Pratt?" Makayla's fearless voice directed them all.

Kimi bowed her head and wondered what Dr. Now-Has-A-Name would say.

"Thank you, Lord, for a chance to attend worship today, and for the beautiful job Makayla did. I hope the words she sang touched others as much as they did me. Please bless this meal to our bodies now. Amen."

Everyone except Kimi reached for their sandwiches. She watched Dr. Pratt take that first bite. The look on his face told her what she needed to know. "I guess he's from Chicago then."

Dr. Pratt smiled around his mouthful of food and nodded. After he swallowed, he looked at Kimi, his brow again furrowed. "Why didn't you ask someone where Mr. Maskey was instead of climbing up on the pew?"

He wasn't going to let it go, was he? "It just seemed easier to climb up and look for him myself. Is it such a big deal?"

Kimi braced herself for a lecture.

His words, though, came out monotone and matter-of-fact. "I suppose not. I'm a rule-follower. It makes me good at my job, but most people find it off-putting."

What was she supposed to make of that? All their stilted conversations came back to her. He'd never been unkind. Even when he'd asked about the pew, he hadn't said anything ugly to her... "You asked why I was up on the pew."

He nodded.

"Why did you ask?"

"Because I wanted to know. I didn't understand why anyone would climb up there."

"Hm." Kimi reached for her sandwich. Had he been asking about the pew out of curiosity instead of judgment? Could it be as simple as that? And if so, what did it say of her that she'd automatically assumed he was judging?

Four

Owen polished off his Italian Beef and sat back in his seat. Thankfully everyone else was still eating, so there was no pressing need to make small talk. He tried to take in the scenery out the window over her left shoulder, but his eyes kept wandering to Kimi.

He'd upset her when he'd asked about the pew. He would call his mother later and relay the conversation. Maybe she could tell him what he'd said that had offended Kimi. He'd definitely said something wrong. She'd gotten quiet, and quiet didn't seem to be a natural state of being for her. He didn't know how he'd messed up, though.

"You two should go to the Fall Festival together. It's always so much fun — you'd have a great time."

Makayla's statement hung over the table like blasting powder after cannon fire.

"Um, I'm sure Dr. Pratt has a busy schedule..." Kimi's words got lost in the smoke.

"Call me Owen."

"Huh?"

"Owen. My name's Owen. You can call me by my given name."

Kimi glanced at Mr. and Mrs. Maskey. "But they call you Dr. Pratt."

"Because that's who I was to them when they met me. Besides, it creates emotional distance."

"Emotional...?"

Owen looked from Mrs. Maskey's stricken face to Kimi's frowning one. "Emotional distance. They need that in case..."

"In case what?" Kimi's voice climbed an octave.

Why was everyone staring at him? "In case something goes wrong with Makayla's treatment. Her parents are her advocates, and they need to keep emotional distance from me so that if something I do doesn't work well for Makayla, they can fight for her. They won't think of me as a friend whose feelings they don't want to hurt. They'll think of me as a doctor, and that'll make it easier for them to stand up to me if they ever need to."

"To fight for Makayla's treatment?" Kimi stared at him, a glint in her eyes.

Owen nodded. "Of course. What did you think I meant?"

Makayla put a hand on Kimi's arm. "She thought you were saying my folks needed emotional distance in case the treatment goes wrong and I die."

"Oh." Owen regarded the four people sharing a table with him. "That's true, too, but that's not what I was trying to say."

Kimi held eye contact with him and nodded. Was that sympathy in her eyes? He'd done it again, hadn't he? Said something people took the wrong way, something that made him an outsider. And Dr. Jameson wanted him to go to a reception with politicians, people who dropped conversational landmines as a hobby?

"Seriously. You two should think about going to the Fall Festival together." Makayla carried on with the conversation as though not a single awkward sentence had been uttered.

Owen peered at the teen. "I'm not sure festivals are my cup of tea."

A snort came from Kimi's general direction before Makayla answered. "That's okay. Kimi prefers coffee."

"She stood on the pew."

Owen's mom *tsked*. "I've stood on a dining room chair before when I've needed help to reach something. How is that any different?"

"That's in your house. Would you go over to someone else's house, pull out one of their dining room chairs, and climb up on it?"

His mom chuckled. "I suppose you have a point there. What if we were at your grandmother's house, though? Or someplace where I felt comfortable and familiar enough to make myself at home?"

Owen grunted. "People aren't supposed to make themselves at home in church, though."

"Are you sure about that?"

The ground shifted under his feet, and Owen decided to back out of the conversation. He wasn't ready to jump into that quicksand yet. "That's not important right now. I need to understand why she got upset when I pointed out that she'd been standing on the pew. It's not like I said something she didn't already know."

Mom exhaled with a half-laugh-half-sigh. "You're not going to dig in your heels and demand that pew-standing be punishable by flogging, are you?"

Owen ran a hand through his hair. "No. Not giving your son the answer he needs, though... Well, no promises there."

"Ha. Nice one." Owen's mom was one of the few people who always knew when he was joking. People generally took him literally. He couldn't blame them, either, since he often did the exact same thing to other people.

"Mom..."

"Very well. You were stating a fact, but your friend Kimi might not know you well enough to realize that. Most people, when they say something of that nature, mean it as condemnation."

"Huh." Owen leaned back in his chair. "Are you sure this isn't just a female thing?"

"I'm pretty sure it applies across the board — men and women."

"So... stating fact is a form of judgment?"

"In social settings like this, yeah, most of the time. For example, if you tell someone their shirt is blue, it's not a big deal. If, however, you tell them their shirt is too small, then you're judging them for being overweight or eating too much or not being able to properly dress."

Owen shook his head. "So when I commented on her pew-standing, what was I saying? I wasn't calling her fat, was I?"

Mom's chuckle gave him hope. "No, not fat. Maybe a sinner or a heathen or something like that, but not fat."

One sentence from his mother, and his hope was dashed. Which was worse? Calling Kimi a heathen or calling her fat?

"Thanks for the help, Mom."

"Are you going to apologize to her?"

"I'm pretty sure I have to if I ever want to see her smile again."

Silence had never been so loud before.

"Uh..." He had meant to keep that last part to himself.

"So this isn't just about getting good coffee then, or a basic social blunder, is it?"

"I..."

His mom's voice dropped. "It's okay. You don't need to give me details until you're ready. I'll be praying for your apology to go well."

He didn't want to put any of it into words anyway. Expressing emotions took effort on his part as it was, but this... Whatever he felt for Kimi was too tenuous. If he said it out loud, it might disappear. "Thanks Mom. I'll talk to you in a couple of days."

"I look forward to hearing how the apology went. Love you."

"Love you, too."

Owen hit the *end* button and slipped his phone into his pocket. Time for coffee. And hopefully a smile.

Owen approached Kimi's kiosk. He'd spent too much time after his talk with his mom arguing with himself about what to say, and as a result, he was behind schedule. Not that she would notice. Nobody but him paid attention to the exact time. She probably hadn't even missed him.

He rounded the last corner only to find Kimi in front of her kiosk and craning her neck in his direction.

Owen picked up his pace, careful to step over the cable protector he'd somehow not seen last week. And the week before.

Kimi's usual grin was in place, but a question lurked in her eyes. "You're late. I began to wonder if you would show."

"I... You know what time I get my coffee?" People didn't usually care enough to take heed of the details.

She reached for the espresso beans. "It took me a few months to realize it, but I eventually caught on. You've been consistent ever since, never off by more than a minute or two."

"I was three minutes late once. A woman was in labor, and her husband was panicked. I found her a wheelchair and helped her into the elevator."

"Labor and Delivery? That's quite a ways away from the surgical waiting room. Where exactly is your office?"

"I'm over in the research wing. Tiny office, but lots of lab space."

"What prompted you to start coming all the way over here for your coffee? That's at least a fifteen-minute walk."

Owen tapped his right foot. "Seventeen unless the stairwell is crowded."

Kimi grinned as she handed him his large half-caff triple nonfat medium whip white mocha. "Why come all this way? I happen to know the kiosks on the other side of the hospital display the same menu as I do."

"I spend too much time in my chair at a desk. The walk over here and back is good for me, and I like your smile. It's worth the extra effort to include that in the start to my day."

Color stole up Kimi's cheeks. "Oh...well..."

"I didn't mean to upset you yesterday."

Her lips dipped down in a frown.

"About the pew."

They dipped lower.

"It might have sounded like I was judging you."

And lower.

"I wasn't, though. Sometimes I state facts and other people hear judgment." He swallowed. "I'm sorry if that happened."

Kimi nodded, and a tentative smile replaced the frown. "In that case, apology accepted."

"Will you go out with me?"

Her eyes widened.

Owen sighed. "That came out wrong."

"So you don't want to take me out?" There she went with that whole rising-an-octave thing again.

He shook his head. "I do, but..." Owen set his coffee down. Thank goodness, no one else was thirsty this morning. "I'm required to attend this reception. I'm supposed to make small talk with the people from the FDA so they'll approve the drug Makayla's getting. I was told to get a tuxedo and a date."

"What happens if you don't?"

No way would Owen answer that question. Even the most socially inept person didn't admit his boss had threatened to hire him an escort if he couldn't score a date for himself.

He did what every educated American does. He sidestepped the question. "It's this coming Thursday evening. Are you available?"

Her eyes filled with laughter, but somehow it didn't feel like she was laughing at him. "I have study group that night, but I might be able to miss it this week."

"What are you studying for?"

"I'm working on an art therapy degree. I'm in the home stretch. Thesis, internship, and all that."

Owen's head tilted to the side of its own volition. "You don't need a study group for a thesis."

"No, but you do need one if you want help preparing for your boards, which I'll be taking as soon as I jump through all the right hoops and officially graduate."

"When will that be?"

She frowned. "I hoped December, but I'm having a hard time getting in enough intern hours, so it'll most likely be next May instead. We'll see."

He'd always suspected there was more to Kimi than a warm smile and hot coffee, but he hadn't known how to ask without sounding like an inept stalker. So he'd stayed quiet. The questions bubbled up inside of him, though. Where was she interning? What was her thesis about? Did she expect her boards to be difficult?

Someone stepped into line behind him, and Owen forced his curiosity into submission in favor of the more immediate need. "Will you think about Thursday?"

She grabbed a napkin from the nearby holder. Pulling the pen from behind her ear, she jotted down a phone number and pushed it across the counter to him. "Call me sometime tomorrow and I'll have an answer for you."

He nodded and turned on his heel. She hadn't said no, and even though he again stumbled over the cable protector, he didn't spill any coffee on his lab coat. The day was getting off to a first-rate start.

Owen arrived back in his office before realizing why his coffee hadn't spilled when he'd tripped. He'd left his cup sitting on the little counter at Kimi's kiosk.

She was definitely going to turn him down. She'd be a fool not to.

Five

A date? With Dr. Owen Pratt? Could she even remember his name? What if she went to this thing and accidentally referred to him as Dr. No-Name?

Kimi helped the next customer as the doctor walked away. A medium Americano, heavy on the cream, no sugar. Easy enough that she could make it with her eyes closed, which is probably why she didn't notice Owen had left his coffee behind until she handed the completed Americano to the woman with dark circles under her eyes.

Oh, well. He'd be back if he wanted it.

Better yet, if he came back, she'd make him a fresh one. That should soften the blow of her rejection, right? Because she definitely wasn't going to this reception with him.

Kimi held her phone in a death grip as she searched her contacts for the number she wanted and clicked the *call* command.

Two rings later, a familiar voice greeted her. "Hello?"

"Owen asked me on a date." Kimi jumped right past the normal niceties of small talk.

"Owen?" Confusion laced Mrs. Maskey's voice.

"Pratt. Owen Pratt."

"Oh my. Makayla will be thrilled."

"I haven't said yes." Kimi picked at her cuticle. "I don't know what to make of him."

Mrs. Maskey chuckled. "Very few people do. The question is, do you like him?"

"Well, I don't know. I think I do, but then he says something that makes me feel like a worm, and then I'm not so sure. Does he talk to everyone that way?"

"Hm." Mrs. Maskey paused before she continued. If Kimi knew her half as well as she thought she did, Makayla's mom was talking to God before speaking to her. "Our opinion of Dr. Pratt is shaped in large part by the fact that, without him — and barring a miracle — our daughter would be dead by now." Only the slightest of cracks traced its way through her words. "So we're biased. I can admit that. When the pharmaceutical company moved him from Chicago to northern Virginia, though, we were thrilled. Makayla likes him, and she's generally a good judge of character."

"She doesn't waste time on people who are fake." Kimi had seen it firsthand. Makayla invested her time in people she deemed real. She ignored most everyone else.

"Precisely," Mrs. Maskey continued. "We didn't even know he was a believer until he showed up in Greg's Sunday School class."

Kimi already knew the story of how Owen had shown up in the class Mr. Maskey taught on Sunday mornings. She'd heard about it from Makayla at the time.

"But... he's kind of odd, right?"

Angela Maskey was the only person Kimi had ever met who could snort and make it sound ladylike. "You know Rylie, right? In Child Life?"

"Yeah. She's one of the supervisors for my internships."

"Talk to her. She works in Pediatric Oncology. She's had more experience with Dr. Pratt than anybody, and she's likely more objective than any of us will be."

A sigh slipped through Kimi's lips. "Okay, but do me a favor and don't mention this conversation to Makayla."

Angela didn't bother masking her chuckle this time. "Not a word, but let me remind you that she does have you two paired off as a couple for the Fall Festival in her mind, and she's not likely to let that go anytime soon."

Kimi shook her head as she said goodbye.

Kimi eyed the digital clock on her cash register as her shift at the coffee kiosk drew to a close the next day. Owen had called once, but she'd let it go to voicemail. She was scheduled in pediatrics that afternoon. She would be leading the children in a simple sketching class with colored pencils. Her internship required a combination of one-on-one meetings and group sessions.

Rylie was supposed to help her set up and get the kids settled in for today's session. If Kimi's replacement would hurry and get to the kiosk, she would be able to make it to the meeting room early. Hopefully, she could get a moment alone with Rylie before the young patients started filing in.

By the time Beatrice came through the doors to the left, Kimi was ready to shout for joy. Of course, it took the woman an extra three minutes to count the cash drawer, but it was finally done. Kimi was off the clock and racing for her destination.

She burst through the door as Rylie clicked the legs of the last child-sized easel into place. "Well hey, Kimi. I didn't expect you for another ten minutes or so. Fifteen kids signed up for today."

"Tell me about Owen Pratt."

Rylie glanced at her, eyebrows drawn together. "Dr. Pratt?"

Great. Now she was as abrupt as he was. "Angela Maskey said I should ask you about him."

Rylie looked behind Kimi to the open doorway before lowering her voice. "Why are you asking about Dr. Pratt?"

Kimi was butchering the conversation, not to mention making a less-than-professional impression on one of the people whose signature was required on her internship paperwork if she ever wanted to graduate. "He asked me on a date. Sort of. He's attending a reception or something, and he doesn't want to go alone. He confuses me, though. Remember me telling you about the odd guy who kept coming to my kiosk?"

"Dr. No-Name, right?"

Kimi nodded. "Turns out that's Dr. Pratt."

Rylie tilted her head to the side. "As I recall, you kind of liked Dr. No-Name. You might not have been thinking about dating him, but you had nothing against him. Or am I missing something?"

"No, you're not. I did like him, just not in a romantic way. Then I went to the Sunday service this past weekend to hear Makayla sing, and I couldn't find the Maskeys after the service let out, so I climbed up on a pew to take a peek around, and..."

Rylie ruffled the hair of a pre-teen who shuffled into the room, IV pole in tow. "You have a class to teach. As long as you don't mind a lot of walking, you can come with me afterward. I have a full schedule, but I can give you the scoop on Dr. Pratt."

More children filed in and took their seats at the fifteen easels as Kimi nodded a grateful agreement to Rylie.

Once the last child took his seat, Kimi took charge of the class. "How's everyone doing?" The answers were mixed and mostly mumbled, but she didn't let that deter her. "Today we're going to learn some of the basics of sketching with colored pencils, but before we get started, I'd like each of you to tell me your name and a sentence or two about what you like to do when you're not stuck here in the hospital."

Art Therapy, at its heart, was about getting people to open up and express what was buried deep inside them. Once those dark corners of the psyche were brought into the light, healing could begin. Sometimes those hidden places revealed themselves through whatever art project they were working on. Other times, words sufficed. One thing was definite, though. Kids rarely opened up at all when you asked them outright about the reason for their hospital stay.

"So, about Owen..." Kimi raced to keep up with Rylie, who hurried toward the MRI room. One of her pediatric oncology kids was scheduled for a scan and having a panic attack. An anesthesiologist would be called in if the Child Life Specialist couldn't calm the girl down.

Rylie hit the button to call up the elevator and turned to Kimi. "The first time I met him, he told me straight up that he had no social skills, and since he's moved his research here and I see him more often, I can say it's completely true."

"That's weird, right? I mean, he's a grown man..."

Rylie shook her head. "Get him to tell you about his schooling, and it might make better sense. He's a good guy, really good, and he cares about these kids. He's no good at small talk, though. If you want him to carry on a conversation, you need to ask meaningful questions. Chitchat about weather, sports, or even politics, though? He has no interest, and you won't get more than a word or two followed by a long stretch of silence."

The elevator door opened, and they were soon being swooped down to the radiology floor. "Do you think he's odd? It feels like I'm the only one who sees that."

Rylie's head bobbed back and forth for a minute before she answered. "We all have quirks. Dr. P's are no stranger than mine or yours. They're just different. Once you get to know his, you'll find yourself working around them, and when you can do that, you'll get to know the man underneath the quirks better."

"Sounds like a lot of work." Kimi's remark fell somewhere between a mutter and a mumble.

"Experience tells me he's worth it, but you're the only one who can make that decision."

The elevator dinged, and Rylie raced through the still-opening doors on her way to the MRI suite. Kimi didn't bother following. She wouldn't be allowed access, and she already had her answer.

"You look lovely."

Kimi smiled, but her lips felt stiff. Her sister-in-law had loaned her a shimmering plum-colored gown covered in sequins. Its modest neckline would come in handy since — at five feet tall in heels — she was short enough to give other people an advantageous view. Any man in the room would be able to peer straight down the front of anything she wore that showed even the slightest hint of cleavage. "That's the thing about being short."

"What?" Owen's eyebrows lifted.

Great. Why couldn't she have whispered inside her own head instead of out loud? "I..."

He tilted his head to the side.

There was nothing for it. She couldn't think up a lie quickly enough, the curse of being raised to value truth. "When you're short and you look in the mirror, you might think you're wearing something that shows just a tiny bit of cleavage. To every man in the room, though, who towers over you, you're showing a lot because they're looking at it from a different angle."

Owen's eyes dropped to the neckline of her gown and then swiftly back up to her eyes. At least color stained his cheeks. She took consolation in not being alone in her embarrassment. He coughed into his hand before speaking. "Are you showing cleavage in this dress?"

Kimi laughed. She couldn't help it. His scrunched-together eyebrows, coupled with the blush that continued to blossom, was too adorable. "No, I'm not. My brother's wife loaned me something to wear. She said it was the highest neckline I'd find without dressing like a grandma."

Owen nodded, his gaze again skimming the front of her gown. "Is she short then, too?"

"Short and reed-thin despite the three rugrats she's brought into this world." Kimi closed her door without bothering to fetch a jacket or shawl. Autumn was just around the corner, but summer was reluctant to let go, and the evening remained just shy of toasty.

49

Owen offered his arm as they left her building and approached his car. "Family's important to you."

She lifted an eyebrow at him, and he shrugged. "It's in your voice. I'm not always oblivious."

"Oh. Yeah. My family... they've always been there for me despite my wild ways."

He closed the door behind her, circled the car, and got in. "Aside from your climbing on church pews, I haven't seen much about you that would tell me you're wild."

Kimi hung her head. Meaningful conversation...wasn't that what Rylie had said?

Six

As Owen pulled away from the curb, Kimi answered the question he hadn't quite asked. "I went out west after high school. I had a scholarship to a fine arts college, and I loved the area so much, I decided not to move back."

"Art school?" Did people actually make a living doing that? "What kind of art?"

One of her shoulders lifted, causing the sequins on her dress to sparkle. "It's hard to get work as an artist. When money got tight, I started hanging out in the tourist areas and sketching people for pay. I enjoyed what I did, and I didn't have any bills to speak of, so it worked for me."

No bills? How was that possible? "Didn't you have rent? Or a phone bill? Something?"

He glanced over at her as he came to a stoplight. Color stole up her cheeks as she shifted in her seat.

"I, uh, lived with a bunch of other artists. Sort of like a co-op. I eventually got my own room, but I still shared a bathroom with a dozen other people."

She never ceased to surprise him. "What made you decide to leave... all that... and pursue an Art Therapy degree?"

51

"I was home visiting my parents one Christmas, and I met the Maskeys at church. Makayla got so excited when she learned I was an artist. She went on and on about the kids in the hospital and how I should volunteer with them and how the occupational therapists used art to help the brain surgery patients redevelop their fine motor skills."

"Makayla's a persuasive kid."

"Yeah. Before I knew it, she dragged me to the pediatric oncology unit so she could introduce me to some of her friends. She talked the nurses into letting me set up my easel and do caricature sketches for fun."

Owen deftly changed lanes to get to the exit he needed as he waited for Kimi to continue.

"A chaplain stopped by to see what all the fuss was about. She had me draw a caricature of her so she could put it up on the bulletin board and give the kids something to laugh about. Pretty soon all the nurses dotted the bulletin board, too. The chaplain — she told me the hospital was thinking about hiring a full-time Art Therapist. She started talking about the job and all the good art therapists can do. Suddenly my whole life in Portland seemed shallow."

"Shallow's not a word I'd use to describe you."

She lifted a delicate shoulder. "I loved it. Don't get me wrong. But that's exactly why I lived that life — because I loved it. I never gave much thought to living for anyone other than myself, you know? I was a believer, had been since I was a kid, but I'd never thought about whether or not God had given me art or if He intended for me to use it in a specific way. My family is pretty traditional, and art is... different. It's hard to explain."

Owen pulled under the portico of the hotel hosting the reception. A valet opened his door, and he circled the car to where Kimi, having also been let out by a valet, stood. He held out his arm to her, and she looped her hand through it.

"Does that bother you? About my art?"

Something in her brown eyes tugged at his heart. She looked uncertain, so unlike the Kimi he'd come to know over his months of coffee-buying. "Should it?"

She looked away. "You said you're a rule-follower, and I've always kind of been a rule-breaker."

His words from the previous Sunday came full circle. They'd made sense when he'd said them, but hearing the remark on Kimi's lips made it sound somehow... less. Like following the rules was undesirable. He was most comfortable within highly structured situations. He avoided people who thrived on disorder and confusion. Kimi, though, wasn't like that. She was completely different from anyone he'd ever been attracted to before. He couldn't be near her without feeling off balance, but... he liked it.

"People who don't follow rules create chaos and lead to anarchy. You are... That is to say... I don't think society is going to collapse because you lived in a co-op for artists."

A smile spread across her pixie-like face. Whew. He'd said the right thing. For now. An entire evening lay in wait, though. He still had plenty of time to blow it.

"It's good to see you. And who might this be?"

Owen shook hands. "Dr. Jameson, this is Kimi. Kimi, Dr. Jameson."

His mentor glanced from Kimi to him and back again before shaking her hand as well.

Owen felt the need to defend Kimi lest Dr. Jameson think he'd hired her to accompany him for the night. "Kimi works at the hospital."

The older man's eyes crinkled at the corners. "Very well. I have some people for you to meet."

Tension coiled through Owen's middle. He should have warned her. He should have told Kimi that he needed her to keep the conversation going and fill in for him when he couldn't think of anything appropriate to say. His pride had gotten the better of him, though, and now the evening stretched out ahead like a horror flick on automatic replay.

Dr. Jameson steered them toward a gathering of five men and women. "Senator Yamada, I'd like you to meet..."

"Kimiko! What are you doing here?"

Owen stood back as Kimi embraced the senator like an old friend, albeit a well-respected old friend. Then she bowed to him and the others in his group before stepping back to stand by his side.

Was Kimi...? Sometimes, depending on the lighting, she looked like she might be Asian. Other times, though, her face held no trace of it.

Her hand on his arm tugged him forward. "Senator, let me introduce you to my friend Owen Pratt. He's a doctor. He created a drug that is treating a special kind of pediatric cancer."

The senator shook Owen's hand while Dr. Jameson swooped in. "Senator Yamada serves on the Health, Education, Labor, and Pensions Committee."

Owen remembered some of Dr. Jameson's coaching. The FDA would need to approve the drug, and the FDA was under the oversight of the HELP Committee.

"It's a pleasure to meet you, Senator. How do you know my date?"

The senator excused himself from the group he'd been talking to and led them to a close grouping of three chairs. Dr. Jameson stood by until Senator

Yamada waved him away. "We're fine here. Go find someone else to persuade."

Once Dr. Jameson left, Senator Yamada turned keen eyes on Owen. "I haven't seen the paperwork yet, but I'm aware Gyermeck Pharmaceuticals will be requesting approval for a new drug that's supposed to do amazing things in the world of pediatric cancer. Dr. Jameson no doubt wants me to be wowed by your knowledge or integrity or some such. So please, by all means, go ahead and impress me."

Owen glanced from the senator to Kimi, who offered him a tremulous smile. "I've meticulously compiled the data that will accompany the New Drug Application. I'm sure you don't need me to tell you everything when you're going to be reading it on the NDA."

The senator leaned back, a light in his eyes. "Very well. Then tell me how you met Kimiko."

Owen glanced at Kimi before looking back at the senator. "She makes good coffee. But I call her Kimi."

Senator Yamada's mouth stretched wide. "Coffee is how I came to know her, too. You're in good company." His eyes bore into Owen. "Are you sure you're not here to persuade me to encourage the FDA to fast track your drug?"

Why had Dr. Jameson insisted he come? "That's probably what I'm supposed to do, but I don't know how. I deal in facts and figures. It's a good drug. If the data doesn't convince you of that, then I have no hope of changing your mind. I'd be much more comfortable answering questions after you've read through the NDA. You need at least a rudimentary understanding of the drug, or nothing I say will make any sense."

The senator nodded. "Those of us on the HELP Committee don't generally see the NDA. We trust the FDA to handle those. Occasionally, we might ask to review one if concerns arise, but those instances are rare."

"Oh." Owen anticipated the lecture from Dr. Jameson. It was sure to come.

"My brother decided to start his own business." Kimi's voice soothed his frazzled nerves, but he still had no idea what she was doing. "Toshihiro loved coffee, and that seemed like the ideal path for him to take."

Owen bided his time. Asking Kimi what she was up to would almost definitely be a social *faux pas*.

"Toshihiro chose to open a coffee truck. You know, like a food truck, but strictly serving high-end coffee. He started that business about the same time I returned home and went back to school. I worked for him in exchange for room and board for the first few years while he got everything off the ground. It was quite a coup when he received a permit to park in front of the Capitol Building. That's where I met Senator Yamada."

The senator rested his arm along the back of his seat. "I still see his truck there, but it's no longer Toshihiro taking my order."

Kimi nodded. "The business grew faster than anyone thought. My brother got contracts to provide coffee in several of the area hospitals. I work there now, at one of the kiosks at Ferito Technology Memorial Hospital. Running his business takes so much time now that Toshihiro rarely gets to wile away his days in a coffee truck. He misses it."

Senator Yamada nodded. "Toshihiro thrives on interacting with people. He's gifted in that way."

Kimi smiled, but her posture stiffened. "He's quite personable, and you're right. That's always served him well."

The senator stared at Kimi.

It was as though the two were having a conversation to which Owen wasn't privy. Their subtext was in a language he didn't understand, and it fascinated him. If he were honest with himself — which he always was — he'd admit that it also made him uncomfortable.

Finally, the senator gave a single nod. "It was good to see you again Kimiko, but I should catch up with a couple of other people here. I'm sure their company won't be nearly as delightful as yours, but nonetheless, duty calls." They all rose, and Senator

Yamada bowed to Kimi then held a hand out to Owen. "I'm not quite sure what to make of you, Dr. Pratt, but Kimiko here doesn't suffer fools lightly. You're worth her time, so you're worth mine. If your NDA gets stuck, contact my office, and I'll take a look at the data."

As soon as the senator stepped away, Owen reached for Kimi's arm. "We need to leave before Dr. Jameson tries to introduce me to someone else. I'm sure the next person won't be as understanding as Senator Yamada."

With grace that belied the force she needed to employ, Kimi removed his hand and tucked her own around the crook of his elbow. "You did fine. I imagine many of these politicians would appreciate someone speaking to them without trying to use them for a change."

"The problem is that I *was* trying to use Senator Yamada. I'm just no good at it."

Kimi pulled him toward a buffet table rather than the exit. "Why aren't you any good at it?"

"I'm not good at being anything other than straightforward. Gyermeck's board insisted I come here, and Dr. Jameson tried to coach me in being persuasive in an understated way." He tugged at his collar with his free hand. "I don't do subtle, though. I don't know how. Most of the time I don't even realize when people are being subtle with me."

Kimi released his arm, and before he could protest, she pressed a plate piled high with hors d'oeuvres into one of his hands. "We'll share. I have the drinks." She waltzed away with two glasses of sparkling lemonade.

She was a godsend. The last thing he needed was to trip and spill a drink on his tuxedo. The food choices she'd picked, too, were all pretty harmless. Cheese, crackers, a few cherry tomatoes. Nothing with sauce on it, and nothing that could drip. Bless her.

Kimi led the way to a dark corner of the large room and sat with her back to the crowd. "Sit beside me so we can share."

He settled onto the settee and balanced the plate between them. "Thank you."

The rest of what he wanted to say fell victim to his knotted-up tongue.

Seven

Kimi glanced at Owen. "For what?"

All she'd done was make sure she got fed before he took her home.

"You picked a spot where we won't be easily found, and you got me food that won't make a mess if spilled."

She shrugged as she plucked a radish from their shared plate. "That's not anything special."

He put a hand on hers before she could pop the vegetable into her mouth. "It is to me. Thank you."

Kimi nodded as she pulled her hand out from under his and slipped the radish between her lips. The shadows were back, turning his eyes from their normal blue into a cloudy grey. She reached out and gave his hand a small squeeze. "You're welcome."

The longer they sat with their backs to the room, the more the tension eased out of Owen's shoulders. Kimi was polishing off the last of her lemonade when Angela Maskey's words came back to her. She was supposed to ask about...

"Where did you go to school?"

Owen set his plate on the cushion to his left. "Growing up, I was mostly homeschooled. My mom put me in public school when I started kindergarten, but by the fourth grade, nobody knew what to do with me. Third grade, really, so starting in the fourth grade, Mom found an online school that suited me better."

Poor kid. "Why didn't your teachers know what to do with you?"

Owen smiled. "It wasn't their fault. My mom says her lightbulb moment was when my third grade teacher called to tell her I'd gotten in trouble for writing in a textbook."

"I didn't know third graders had textbooks."

He chuckled. "Yeah, that was where the lightbulb came in. A high schooler left his algebra book on the bus, and I thumbed through it. One of the examples they gave was solved incorrectly, so I fixed it. In pen."

Kimi covered her mouth. "Oh dear. So you're a genius or something, aren't you?"

"It depends on your definition. If you're using the IQ standard, then yes."

Some people might have blushed at her off-hand comment, but not Owen. Unless she was reading him wrong, he'd heard the literal question, not flattery. "So how old were you when you finished high school?"

"I could have completed the schoolwork and required credits by fourteen, but my parents didn't let me graduate till I was sixteen. Then, when I started college, I did my first two years online."

"Hm." Should she push for more? "Was it that they didn't want you to lose your childhood, or that they didn't want to miss out on it themselves?"

Owen's eyes widened for the briefest second. "That's astute of you. I suppose it was a little of both."

Kimi sat her glass on the floor. "So, did you take four years to finish college? How long did you actually live on campus?"

Owen again tugged at his collar, a sure sign that their conversation made him uncomfortable. "I enrolled in med school at eighteen. By the time I finished my residency in pediatric oncology, I knew I didn't have the people skills to treat kids on a regular basis. And I'd gotten this idea for a new drug."

"Huh." Was he trying to sidestep her question? "So you're a doctor-doctor. I thought you were just a research doctor. You know, a PhD, but not a medical doctor."

"I, uh, went back to school and got a second doctorate. Biochemistry and molecular genetics."

Kimi stuttered out a, "Wow," but didn't know what to say beyond that. She kind of liked the guy, but what would they ever talk about?

"So how did you end up working for Gyermeck?"

Owen looked over his shoulder before answering. "Post-graduate studies are all about money. Schools only take a limited number of doctoral candidates on at a time, and then they make the degree program stretch out as long as possible so they can collect as much money as possible. In most fields, molecular genetics included, the longer you're at the university, the more they can profit off you. Everything you invent or design while you're a student becomes property of the university. I didn't want to spend the next ten years jumping through collegiate hoops and having nothing to show for it. I knew if I got grant money to fund my research, I could more or less write my own ticket — or at least keep above the fray. So I tracked down Dr. Jameson. I'd taken a class from him in med school, but he'd since left academia for what was rumored to be a lucrative position with Gyermeck."

"So Dr. Jameson is a friend of yours then?"

"Kind of. A bit of a mentor, a bit of a colleague. I like to think he's protecting my best interests, but I'm not foolish enough to pretend he's not also looking out for Gyermeck's bottom line. He believed in the concept I pitched to him, but if he gave me a blanket grant, the university would still own the end product. So he put the Gyermeck lawyers to work, and they came to an agreement with the university. Gyermeck would own everything I created, but the protocol I employed to create it would be owned corporately between the two."

"I don't understand. If your research went with you when you graduated, how does owning the protocol help the university?"

"There's a strong chance the method I used will be effective in developing cancer-fighting drugs to target other forms of the disease."

Kimi sat back in her seat. That was huge. Crazy huge. How many people in in America alone suffered with cancer? With the university using Owen's protocol to potentially create other new cancer drugs, they stood to make millions of dollars, maybe even billions, especially if they could target the more common cancers. "That's okay with you? The university profiting from your work?"

He shrugged. "That's the way the business goes. Besides, once the FDA approves this drug, I'll be able to move on to another one. The next cancer I'd like to go after isn't on the list of ones my alma mater is currently targeting."

"You could change the world."

He drained the last of his lemonade. "Maybe the Maskeys' world and the worlds of families like them. That's good enough for me."

Kimi peeked back at the ballroom in time to catch Dr. Jameson zeroing in on them. She grabbed Owen's hand and darted to her right. "Come on, let's make a run for it."

EIGHT

Owen followed along behind Kimi as she tugged him toward an unobtrusive exit near the room's bar. A couple of waiters stood outside smoking. He started to wave his hand in front of his face as Kimi asked them which way would take them back to the valet stand. Then she darted down the sidewalk, his hand still in hers. "Follow me"

In less than five minutes, they approached a valet, and Owen fished the ticket out of his tuxedo pocket. His car was brought around, and they climbed in.

"Dr. Jameson will not thank me for leaving early. He had specific people he wanted to introduce me to."

"Senator Yamada liked you, and that's what matters."

"Why does he matter so much? He doesn't control what the FDA permits or doesn't permit. Besides, the data backs up the drug's efficacy. They can't *not* approve it."

"You played the game in order to get your second PhD, but you don't know how to play it now...?"

"Is that what I did? Play a game? I saw the obstacles and made a plan to circumvent them."

"Maybe 'game' isn't the right word, but this isn't any different. Is it?"

Owen cast a glance her way as he merged onto the freeway. "What you say makes sense, but it feels different. Why?"

He kept his eyes on the road, but he caught Kimi watching him in his peripheral vision.

"Well, when you went to Dr. Jameson about getting funding for your research, you were asking him to believe in you. This time, you're asking strangers to believe in something you created. That makes it different. Kind of like a parent. 'You can say whatever you want to say about me, but don't you dare say anything bad about my kid.'"

"In your analogy, the drug would be my child?"

"I don't know. You tell me."

Owen eased off the freeway and merged back into traffic on the surface streets. "Is this the therapy part of your art therapy degree coming to the fore?"

Her laughter sparkled in the confines of the car. "Maybe. But the question still stands."

"When my work was on the line, anything I did reflected on me, and I was fine with that. Once a drug is sent out into the world, though, people can misuse it. In their misuse, though, the results will still reflect on me. I created this drug to change lives for the better. If I ruin the drug's chances, it won't be able to do what I designed it to do. It won't save lives, and it'll be my fault because I'm lousy at small talk."

Owen slipped his car into a parking spot and turned to Kimi. "Does that make sense?"

Kimi tucked a stray hair behind her ear. "Perfectly. And you might be right. Maybe it's better to let the drug speak for itself."

She picked at a cuticle instead of reaching for her seat belt.

"Why do I feel like I'm missing something? What aren't you saying?" His heart sped up its pace the second she turned her eyes on him.

"It's nothing bad. I just wonder if it parallels our relationship with God a little. He wants us to go out into the world to make an eternal difference, right?"

Owen nodded. "We mess up, though, and it reflects poorly on Him."

Kimi chuckled. "Of course, as the drug's creator, that puts you on par with God, and I'm not saying that. It's an interesting juxtaposition, though, don't you think?"

He swallowed. "Interesting, yes, but my drug doesn't have free will. And in this case, if it's prevented from doing its job, the blame will rest squarely on its creator."

"It's probably for the best, then, that you're not one of those doctors whose ego tells him he's a god."

Owen had met more than a few of those during his tenure. "Definitely."

Silence settled around them, but it was the comfortable kind, and Owen was in no hurry to end the evening. "Can I ask a question.?"

She tipped her head the tiniest bit to the side. "Sure."

"Senator Yamada called you Kimiko."

One corner of her mouth tilted up. "I didn't hear a question."

Of course not. He knew better than that. "Which is your birth name, and which is the nickname?"

"Kimiko is the name on my birth certificate. It means *child without equal.* When I left home, I shortened it to Kimi, which means *she who is without equal.* My family, however, insists on calling me Kimiko. My mother says that if I ever want her to honor my wish to be called Kimi I need to marry and have kids. Then I will stop being the child."

Owen covered his mouth but not quickly enough to hide his smile. "So do you prefer Kimi or Kimiko?"

"Kimi, please. If I'd ever wanted you to call me something different, I would have said so."

Direct. He could live with that. "Is it okay if I walk you up?"

She pulled her bottom lip in between her teeth for just a second before releasing it again. "Very well."

He climbed from the car and opened her door. "I don't plan to stay. It's the polite thing to do. Seeing you safely to your door, that is."

"Ah. Safety first and all that."

They reached Kimi's door, and she withdrew a key from her small purse and slid it into the lock. "Thank you for a lovely evening."

"Was it lovely?"

She studied him, and he learned what it felt like to be on the wrong side of the microscope lens. "I enjoyed myself. It was good to see Senator Yamada again, and I had fun getting to know you, too. I think that means it was lovely. Do you not agree?"

He shouldn't have asked the question. He hadn't meant any insult by it, but the way her lips pouted said he'd missed the mark. "You're lovely, and I spent the evening with you, so, yes, I suppose that makes it a lovely evening even though I would have rather done without the fancy clothes or strangers who have no real interest in me."

Kimi graced him with a smile before she pushed her door open.

Owen turned to go but then pivoted back to face her. "I have a trip to LA to check on some patients. I won't be in for coffee tomorrow. I usually plan any trips for Tuesdays and Thursdays, but the scheduling for this one couldn't be avoided."

She tilted her head to the side, the smile still dancing along the corners of her mouth. "I'll miss seeing you."

Owen returned from his trip late Saturday night. A vague message from his pastor awaited him on his home voicemail. Something about a favor.

Hm. Specifics would have been helpful.

Thank goodness, Owen wasn't the type to be easily daunted. He could do almost anything. As long as they didn't ask him to work with children. Or teach adults. Or do anything related to grounds and maintenance. Greeting people was pretty much beyond him, too. They wouldn't want him helping at the coffee counter, either, unless they had a dry cleaning budget.

Feet dragging, Owen entered the foyer Sunday morning and made his way toward the church's office. A receptionist was stationed there during service times in case someone got lost or needed help while everyone else was busy in the sanctuary.

"Pastor Fitzgerald wanted to see me. He said to catch him sometime this morning."

Barbi, according to her nametag, nodded to him. "Are you Mr. Pratt?"

It had taken a few years, but he'd eventually realized people found it arrogant when he corrected them about his title, so he didn't do that anymore. "Yes, that's me."

The woman pulled an envelope from a pile in front of her and handed it to him. "Pastor Fitzgerald needs someone to serve on a committee. The details are in here. He thinks you're a good fit and hopes you'll accept. He also wanted me to make sure you understood it's temporary. The woman whose place you'll be taking went into pre-term labor and has been put on bedrest and ordered to minimize all stress in her life. And..."

Owen managed a smile. "Church committees and low stress don't always go together."

Barbi returned his smile with one fifty watts brighter. "Exactly. I know the pastor would really appreciate you doing this."

He tapped the envelope on the countertop. "I'll read through it later today." Better not to make a commitment before he understood what all it entailed.

Nine

Kimi watched the door. Four of the committee members, herself included, were present and accounted for. Pastor Fitzgerald had told her he would find a fifth person to fill their vacancy. They could muddle along for a little while with only four members, but as soon as they hit a tie vote on something, they'd be in trouble. Her job was to chair this committee and keep it moving forward. So far, she'd managed not to let their progress get mired down in church politics or differing viewpoints, but without that fifth vote, she wasn't sure how much longer that would last.

The door creaked open a couple of inches, and she inhaled deeply. Hopefully the person would at least be familiar with the Fall Festival.

She didn't realize she was holding her breath until Owen came into view and the air rushed out of her lungs. "Are you my fifth?"

The newcomer stared at her, his brows drawn together, before glancing around the table at the other attendees. He held up the envelope in his hand. "Pastor Fitzgerald asked me to help on a committee for the church's Fall Festival. Am I in the right place?"

Everyone except Kimi welcomed him, and Owen slipped into a chair. The puzzled expression didn't leave his face, though, even after Kimi called the meeting to order.

Ninety minutes later, the three other committee members filed out of the room. Owen remained at the table, thumbing through the copious notes he'd taken.

Kimi put all her papers back into their file folder before she sat back down, folded her hands, and rested them on the table. "I didn't mean to sound ungrateful when you arrived. You took me by surprise."

"You're a member of church here."

She nodded. Obviously, her initial reaction didn't bother him. "I joined shortly after moving back home."

"But you stood on a pew."

Not that again. "I thought I explained my reason."

"You explained, but I've been a member here for almost eight months, and I've never seen you. When you stood on a pew to find someone, I thought maybe you hadn't been to church before. You know, that you'd come just to hear Makayla sing. That's not true, though. You're a church member, and I assume that means you're a believer. Yet you work on Sundays, and prior to last week, I'd never once seen you here. I don't understand."

Not that she'd ever made a practice of doing so, but she was definitely never going to stand on a pew again. Besides, wasn't that supposed to be behind them? She let a sigh out and hoped it didn't sound as irritated to his ears as it did to hers. "I am a believer, but we must attend different services."

"Oh." Owen's mouth turned down at the corners.

"You're aware the church offers a couple of different service times, right?"

He nodded and blinked at her. "I don't approve of that."

Kimi closed her eyes. She'd thought they were on their way to a friendship, but if he couldn't accept something like this... "There's nothing sinful about Saturday church, even when it's a contemporary service."

"I..." His voice trailed off before he completed his thought. He stared at his finger nails.

"Owen, look at me."

He raised his eyes to meet hers.

"Do I look like a devil-worshiping heathen?"

He gave his head a small shake.

"The world is made up of lots of different types of people. It's okay that we don't all express our love for God in exactly the same way."

He stood to go, but Kimi still wasn't sure if she'd helped or hurt matters, and she was almost too tired to care. Back to business, then. "The Fall

Festival is in six weeks. Can you continue to serve on the committee for the duration? We meet every Sunday."

He looked over his shoulder at her and nodded. "I don't approve of meeting on Sunday, but I'll keep my commitment."

She ran a hand through her hair, fluffing it as she went. "I work all day Saturday and Sunday. I attend the Saturday night worship service, and the remainder of the week I'm either in school, working, or studying. Sunday's the only evening that's consistently available for this."

Frown lines appeared on his forehead. "What happened to having a day of rest? To keeping the Sabbath holy?"

"It's only for a season. One of my brother's weekend employees quit unexpectedly, and nobody else wants weekends in the surgical waiting room. There aren't a lot of weekend surgeries scheduled, so the tips can be lousy. Last week when I came to the Sunday morning service, my brother gave up his Sunday at church to cover part of my shift for me. It's not perfect, but it's the best either of us can do right now."

Owen nodded and walked out the door.

Kimi slapped her hand down on the tabletop. If only she could tell what was going on behind those eyes of his. Not knowing where she stood with him left her unsettled.

She had a sinking feeling that she needed to apologize again, but she didn't entirely understand why.

Owen wasn't like other people. The whole standing-on-the-pew debacle ought to have taught her that much. Benefit of the doubt only got her so far. She could give it freely, but it still wouldn't tell her what was wrong.

Maybe he wasn't passing judgment on her Saturday church attendance, but if not, why did he seem so put out by her?

Ten

Owen approached the last corner before Kimi's kiosk with trepidation. He peeked around the edge of the wall. She was with a customer, so he stepped back out of view. After counting to fifty, he took another look.

She was alone this time, and he made his approach.

"Good morning." Hesitation shaped her smile, and the fault was his.

He nodded to her. "Good morning. It's supposed to rain today."

She chuckled. "That's what people keep telling me. Do you want the usual?"

"No. I'd like to try something different."

Kimi's left eyebrow climbed high. "Oh? What can I get you then?"

Owen avoided eye contact by studying the display of straws. "It's recently come to my attention. Again. That I can be somewhat rigid in my routine. Because I'm rigid in my routine, people sometimes end up with the impression that I'm a rigid person, maybe even unforgiving. I'm not, though. I just..."

Kimi reached across the counter and lightly touched the back of his hand. "Apology accepted. Now what would you like to drink?"

Warmth pooled in his middle. "What do you recommend?"

Kimi eyed her inventory before answering. "What would you say to a dulce de leche bon bon. I'll make it a triple half-caff."

Owen took a deep breath and released the air from his lungs. "I trust you."

Sunshine broke through on Kimi's face, and she set to work on the contraption she used for making her drinks. "The price hike went into effect, so it'll be $3.85."

He was prepared for the increase. Not knowing exactly how much it would be, though, he'd been carrying extra change with him in anticipation ever since she'd first mentioned it to him. He liked being prepared. With precise movements, he set his money right next to the cash register on the small counter of the kiosk.

A couple of minutes later, she handed him a hot drink. "A bon bon is separated. It's layered like a black and white, but without any alcohol. You have coffee at the top and dulce de leche at the bottom. To mix the two flavors, you just stir."

He took the cup from her and peeked through the lid at the dark coffee within. "This isn't on your menu."

She shrugged. "The menu is to help the people who don't know what they want. We're equipped to make almost anything, but if we listed all the options, people would be overwhelmed and would quit before they even ordered."

Owen took a sip and tried not to pucker at the strong espresso.

Kimi passed a stirring stick to him. "Stir it. It'll make all the difference."

"Why don't you stir it before you serve it?"

"Some people like that first shot of straight espresso. I never know, so I just leave it. In restaurants, this sort of drink is served in a clear glass mug so you can see the separated layers. It makes for a visually impressive drink. Fun, too."

Owen removed the lid and swirled the wooden stirrer through his beverage. The thick dulce de leche rose up from the bottom and changed the color of the espresso. Before putting the lid back on, he raised it to his lips and took another sip. "Wow."

"Good wow or bad wow?"

He tossed the stirring stick into the small garbage bin and fitted his lid onto its cup. "I decided I should start getting a new coffee drink each Monday to broaden my horizons and increase my comfort level with trying new things. I might not want to try anything else after this, though. This might be my new permanent drink."

Kimi's eyes sparkled.

Owen lifted his cup in salute to her before he started to turn away.

"Wait."

He turned back. The smiling confident Kimi of a minute ago was gone. The hesitant Kimi had returned in her place.

"Would you like to go to the Saturday evening service with me sometime?"

"Ah..." His stomach twisted.

"You don't have to answer now. You can think about it. Just let me know by Friday. Or even Saturday. You have my number."

Owen took another drink of his coffee before speaking. "Why are you asking me?"

Kimi's bottom lip disappeared between her teeth for a second. "I'm not sure if you're against it because you think church should only be on Sunday or because it's different from what you're used to. Either way, I think you should attend before making up your mind about it. That's scientific, isn't it? Test a hypothesis and all that. You can't just assume you know something."

Owen felt the corner of his mouth creep up. She was a pure delight when she talked science. "I'll get back to you by Friday."

Her smile stretched wide again. "Good. In the meantime, enjoy your coffee."

He walked away, this time watching for that cable protector across the floor. The bon bon was worth the extra care.

Saturday evening arrived, and Owen still couldn't believe he was going through with this. He'd told Kimi he would, though. So he had to. Didn't he?

Owen had given the whole thing quite a bit of thought since Kimi's invitation. Saturday night itself didn't trip him up. Lots of biblical scholars disagreed on the matter of when church should meet. He'd never bothered to learn Greek or Hebrew, let alone Aramaic, so he wasn't qualified to go back to the original texts and try to decipher the significance of Sunday in the church model.

So Saturday itself wasn't the problem. It was different, though, and different wasn't his happy place.

The idea of a contemporary worship service, on the other hand... Well, that made his jaw clench.

His father thought it good for him to broaden his church horizons. When Owen had called to talk to him about it, Dad had even chuckled and told him, "If you hate it, you can go right back the next day for the service you're used to." Always looking on the bright side of things, his dad.

What did contemporary even mean? No piano? No hymns? Would the preacher approach the pulpit as fireworks went off and a fog machine filled the front of the sanctuary?

Owen took a deep breath as he sat in his car in the church's parking lot. Kimi needed to come straight from work and had wanted to drive herself. Not that he had to drive her. It wasn't a date. Was it? Did anyone go to church for a date? Maybe more people should. It couldn't hurt to start a relationship off with common ground. If this was a date, then she'd asked him. He shook his head. She'd have told him if it was a date... Right?

Kimi approached the building's front doors. Jeans and a loosely fitted sweater were accompanied by calf-high boots. He wasn't sure if the look was supposed to be dressy or casual. No clue there about whether or not this was a date. Regardless, the outfit emphasized her petite form in all the right places.

Owen shook the thought away and got out of the car.

The service wouldn't matter at all if he spent the whole time wrapped up in thoughts of the woman who made his coffee. God. He was at church to focus on and learn about God. Not Kimi. He could do this. After all, it was not a date.

Eleven

Kimi spotted Owen as he stepped into the foyer. He didn't look much different from every time she'd seen him at the hospital Dress slacks, loafers, and a button-down shirt. He'd refrained from wearing his lab coat, of course. She waved to him with her bulletin and smiled as he approached. "Glad you made it."

"I said I would."

She had decided not to take offense at anything Owen said tonight. The more she got to know him, the more she realized he simply had an abbreviated way of communicating. He didn't bother with any of the niceties most people employed. It sometimes made him seem unfeeling, but he wasn't. He just didn't express his feelings the way other people did. She would give him the benefit of the doubt tonight, no matter what he said.

They sank into a pew, and Owen thumbed through the bulletin. "They don't list hymn numbers on here."

Kimi answered in a whisper to match his volume. "Most of these songs aren't in the hymnal. Besides, they'll put the lyrics up on the screen."

"How do people know the harmony?"

"I'm not sure it matters. In all the years I used a hymnal, I never knew what harmony was. I'm not singing any differently now than I did then. I just follow the worship team and remember I'm singing to God, not to the people around me."

Owen frowned but didn't comment further. He turned back to his bulletin and appeared to read it from beginning to end. With the exception of the song titles, the Saturday bulletin was practically identical to Sunday morning's. Did he read that one as thoroughly? Or was he searching for some hidden message to discredit the Saturday evening contemporary service?

"All right everybody! Please rise to your feet. Let's lift our voices to the Father."

A cheer went up around the sanctuary at the worship leader's words. Kimi jumped up and watched out of the corner of her eye as Owen rose more slowly.

When the lyrics to their first song shone on the screen, Kimi clapped in delight. It was one of her favorites. The electric guitar played a riff followed by a brief drum solo before the instruments blended seamlessly together and the singers began pouring their hearts out via words sent soaring to the heavens.

Owen stood stiffly beside her, but as the music continued, his stance softened. Toward the end, she heard his voice in her right ear. The song appeared to be new to him, but he made an effort to participate, and that mattered. Inviting him hadn't been a mistake as she'd first feared.

A couple songs later, Pastor Fitzgerald stepped up on stage and began praying over the service. "Lord, I ask humbly for You to touch the hearts of everyone here. Show them Your will, Your way, and Your love. Use me tonight, Lord, as we tackle some difficult topics."

Amens echoed around the sanctuary as people began sitting back down in their pews. Owen pulled his Bible into his lap while Kimi retrieved her phone and scrolled through to her notetaking app. The verses would be up on the screen, so she never bothered to look them up on her Bible app. She did better with the notes. If a verse came up that she wanted to study more later, she could jot it down rather than searching for it right then. Everybody did it differently, but that system worked best for her.

Owen might not be so agreeable. He glanced at her phone and frowned, but he returned his attention to the front without saying anything.

Everyone filed from the sanctuary out into the foyer. Pastor Fitzgerald stood at one set of double doors and shook people's hands. With multiple other exits, though, people could make their escape without coming face-to-face with the pastor. Kimi always chuckled a bit when she saw people so obviously trying to avoid him.

Personally, she liked to take the extra thirty seconds to thank him for bringing them a message. His sermons gave her something to think about, and they drove her back into God's Word, too, which was a nice bonus.

Pastor Fitzgerald gave Kimi a warm smile as he shook her hand. Then he turned to the next person in line, and surprise lit his face. "Owen, it's good to have you tonight. You're usually here on Sunday, right?"

Owen mumbled a reply Kimi couldn't hear. It must have been about her, though, because Pastor Fitzerald's gaze went from Owen to her with lightning speed. "I see..."

Heat climbed into Kimi's cheeks, and she made a point of studying her shoes as she waited for Owen to finish talking to the pastor.

Owen rested his hand on the small of her back and led her toward the next set of doors and out into the crisp evening air. A hand to the back was a little on the familiar side, wasn't it? But this was Owen, the personification of proper etiquette. He couldn't mean anything by it. Could he?

Ugh. Uncertainty tied her stomach up in knots. She didn't like not knowing where she stood with another person.

As soon as they got away from the crush of people leaving the service, he released her. Ah. He'd only been exercising his gentlemanly character again. So, then, why did her skin tingle where his hand had rested?

"I'm glad you could come tonight. What did you think of it?"

Owen stared off across the parking lot. "The music was loud, and I wish he'd have told people to look the verses up in their Bibles, but Pastor Fitzgerald's sermon was as sound as ever. I assumed the contemporary service had a different pastor."

"He has a couple of protégés, people who are going through seminary or who feel God calling them to the ministry. Every now and then Pastor Fitzgerald will let one of them preach. It's mostly just him, though."

"Hm."

Kimi didn't know whether to say goodnight and be on her way or invite him somewhere for coffee. Her budget was hurting, and she probably shouldn't splurge...

"Care to join me for dinner?" Owen's voice had lost its customary stiffness.

"My rent's due, and I missed part of last Sunday, so money's a little tight."

Owen's eyesbrows drew together. "Do you need money?"

Heat rushed to Kimi's face. "No, I didn't mean that. I just... I'm fine. I'd love to join you. I just don't have any extra money to eat out."

"Oh." Owen didn't say anything else.

"I guess I should get going then..."

"I wouldn't have asked if I didn't intend to pay. I'm sorry I didn't make that clear. Is that not normal? In any event, the offer still stands."

His blue eyes bore into hers and left her feeling bared and exposed like a specimen. She was being tested, but why? Did he think her claim of budget woes was an excuse to avoid dinner with him? "If you're sure it's not a problem, then yeah, I'd like that."

He gave a single nod, but his eyes softened, belying the briskness of his movement. "Good then. Do you want to drive yourself? Or I could drive us both and drop you off back here for your car afterward."

"I guess that depends on where we're going...?"

"One of the ICU nurses recommended a fifties diner around the corner. I haven't had a chance to try it yet, but if she can be believed, they have the best fries in Virginia."

Kimi nodded. "I know the place. I'll ride with you, and you can drop me off back here afterward."

Owen was quiet, but he held out his arm to her, and she looped her hand through it.

Twelve

They settled into their booth, and Owen found himself at a loss. This is where training in small talk would come in handy. Not that he'd be able to remember any of it while across the table from Kimi. He could try, though.

"So tell me about this Fall Festival. Even after sitting in on the committee meeting last week, I'm not entirely sure what we're doing."

Kimi dove into the subject. "The Fall Festival is the second Saturday in October. It's sort of like a county fair, but church sponsored. It's our biggest community outreach event of the year. We have a hay bale maze, rows of booths with games for the kids, face painting, bouncy houses, and even a Ferris wheel."

"It sounds like a child's dream come true."

Her chin tipped up by the slightest degree. "We reach out to adults, too. We set up a tent and have performers throughout the day. Most of the mini-concerts are by our worship team, but some southern gospel singers come in, too. This year we even got one of the local radio stations to partner with us. They'll be broadcasting live from the festival. That should give us a lot of extra publicity."

"How is it an outreach to the community? So far you've described exactly what you said — a county fair."

"We run ads on all the local stations we can afford, including the secular ones. We put coupons in the local newspapers, too. We do everything we can to make sure northern Virginia knows we're here and that we want to help them. People who come to the festival leave with information about our food pantry, thrift store, and other community support services. They learn about our worship times, the programs we have for their kids, and what we do to support missionaries."

"Does the church get new members from doing all this?" He doubted it. These sorts of events didn't historically boost membership.

Kimi shook her head. "But that's not the goal. When people have something to deal with in their life that makes them start to think about God and church, we want them to remember that we're here. There's nothing special about the date. People don't magically realize their need for God on the second Saturday of October. That comes later. In November and December when money's tight and they're having trouble putting a meal on the table. Or in January when a child gets sick and they want someone to come to the hospital and pray. Or February when a parent dies and they have a funeral to plan."

She was obviously passionate about it, and he understood her point, but he still wasn't convinced it was the most effective use of the church's funds. He kept that thought to himself, though.

Barely stopping to breathe, Kimi continued. "By reaching out to people in October and making sure they know we're here, when the hard times come for them, they'll remember us and turn to us for help and support. It's in those moments, when we meet people in their place of darkest, deepest need that we can most effectively minister to them. The big party in October is just a way of planting seeds so people know we're here when those times happen."

"Feeding people — like giving them a turkey for Thanksgiving — how is that a kingdom-growing ministry?"

Kimi sighed as she looked over the menu. "I don't pretend to understand all the theology behind it, and I'm not sure I could hold my own in a debate on the subject, but I know we're called to serve people and that our service should be without condition. We shouldn't be willing to serve only those people who accept Christ on the spot. We should serve people, period. And each time we do — and let them know it's coming out of a heart for Christ — then we're doing what we're supposed to. Don't tell me you disagree."

Owen held up his hands. "I'm not trying to criticize. I'm only curious."

She ran her fingers through her short hair, leavings spikes in her hand's wake. "We try to build relationships with the people who come to us for help. Sometimes it works, and sometimes it doesn't, but if we can create an atmosphere where people feel safe coming to us no matter what baggage they have, then we're creating an atmosphere where we can share the good news with them, where we can impact their lives in an eternal kind of way. It may not be perfect, but it's more than any other church I've ever been to is doing, and I like that I get to be a part of it."

The waitress approached, and they placed their orders. Once she left, Owen picked up the conversation. "The event you've described sounds huge. Are you sure a committee of five is enough to pull it off?"

Kimi chuckled. "I coordinate the big picture, but each of our committee members heads up their own subcommittee and team. Bill is in charge of lining up volunteers for the festival. June takes care of getting all the booths organized and lined up. Jezzie coordinates all the musical performances plus the Ferris wheel and bounce houses."

"What about the woman I replaced? What was her job?"

"Linda was responsible for food. Several food trucks come to the event, plus we have a bake sale that raises money to offset the cost of youth and children's camp during the summer."

Owen frowned. "Should I be doing something? I wasn't aware I needed to do anything beyond show up and be a tie-breaker."

Kimi sat back as the waitress placed their meals on the table. "I took over her duties. I was already in the loop and knew where she was at, so it was easy. Honestly, as long as you can keep us from getting into a deadlock and be there on Festival day to help keep me sane, I don't want to ask anything more from you. Your willingness to step in at the last minute is huge, and we all appreciate it."

Owen started to bow his head and then stopped himself. Some habits were so ingrained he didn't think beyond them. "Would you like to pray?"

Kimi rewarded him with a half-smile. "I'd be honored." She bowed her head, and he followed suit. "Thank You, Lord, for a fabulous church service and for the conversation and company that has followed. Help us to honor You even when we can't see the end game. Amen."

That may have been the shortest prayer Owen had ever heard, but then... He chuckled.

"What's so funny?"

Owen shook his head.

"You can't laugh and then not tell me why."

He tugged at his shirt collar. "Your prayer was shorter than I'm used to, but you're on the short side, so it fit."

Mirth danced in Kimi's eyes as she reached for her fork. "Only a tall person would tell a joke like that, and only a short person would truly appreciate it."

He'd just taken a bite of his burger — sans ketchup, mustard, and mayonnaise to reduce the risk of embarrassing himself in front of Kimi and giving even more money away to his dry cleaner — when Kimi asked, "So do you think you'd ever try Saturday evening service again?"

Owen chewed and swallowed the bite he'd taken. "I still prefer Sunday morning, but if I ever had a reason to be at Saturday's service again, I'd go."

"Hm. Maybe I'll have to make sure you have a reason then."

Thirteen

"All right people. I call this meeting to order." Kimi glanced from the clock on the wall to the people waiting on her to speak. "No new business for tonight, so we'll just go around the table and let everyone give a status report. As we're doing that, tell me what I can do to help you. Can you go ahead and start us off, Jezzie?"

The middle-aged mother of four teen boys, her face lined with fatigue, nodded. "I overbooked our music tent. We typically receive so many rejections that I put out extra inquiries back at the outset. Now I'm getting more positive responses than I'm used to. It's a good problem, I guess, but I feel bad because the worship team already committed to a certain number of time slots, and I need to cut those back."

Kimi made a note in her phone. She would touch base with the worship team to make sure nobody's feelings were hurt. "I'm sure it'll be fine. Maybe they can pitch in and help out elsewhere during their free time. Speaking of... How are we looking where the volunteers are concerned, Bill? Do we have enough people?"

Bill could pull off a good, solid glower without even trying. "We never have enough, and you should know that by now. This year's no different."

This was the third year Kimi had worked with Bill on the Fall Festival. Bill was the personification of pessimism. She'd seen glimmers of change in him, though, and could only hope those changes would see them all through the next several weeks. "Can I do anything to help?"

The retired sheet metal worker shook his head. "I've spoken with all the Sunday School teachers. Most of them are going to let me stop in their classes over the coming month and take five minutes or so to talk about the festival and to pass out a volunteer sign-up sheet. If we're still short after that, I'll start contacting the small groups. I haven't been to the youth group yet, either. A lot of them usually sign up and use it for the community service hours they need for school."

Her optimism bubbling up, Kimi addressed Bill. "Excellent plan. Do you know what you'll do if you make it through all those steps and still don't have the volunteers we need?"

"Ask Pastor Fitzgerald to give it a push from the pulpit. And pray."

Kimi jotted down a few more notes in her phone before returning her gaze to Bill. "Let's not think of prayer as our hail Mary pass."

Bill took his pocketknife out and started cleaning under his nails. "I didn't mean it that way, but point taken."

"How are the booths coming along, June?"

The twenty-something third grade teacher beamed. "We have forty-two booths scheduled. That's ten more than last year."

"Now wait a minute," Bill interrupted. "Nobody told me I needed to get more volunteers for extra booths. And what about the food trucks? Your booths will block them so they can't get in. Let alone the Ferris wheel."

Kimi held up a hand to silence the outburst. "Forty-two is definitely more than we're used to. Have you looked over the event blueprint to make sure there's room for the added booths?"

June leaned forward, elbows braced on the table, a frown marring her porcelain skin. "I didn't think of that. Have I messed things up?"

The booths were always set up back-to-back in a single row so kids could travel up one side and then down the other to hit all the games. Squeezing ten more booths into their normal space would indeed cross over into the area occupied by the food trucks. At a minimum, the booths would block the walkway and the fire marshal would shut them down.

Kimi quickly took notes in her phone before looking back at June. "Email me the dimensions again and a list of what each booth will be doing for their game. I'll go over it and see if I can find a solution. We'll address it again next week. In the meantime, though, don't add any more booths."

"I'm sorry." June clenched her pen so hard it should have snapped. "I didn't mean to make a mess of things."

Kimi would have stretched across the table to pat the woman's hand, but she was too short to reach. "Don't worry about it. We still have plenty of time to iron out any wrinkles. If it were the night before the festival and you were springing ten extra booths on me, then we'd have a problem. This? This is something to be excited about, so don't stress."

She leveled a look at Bill, too. He frowned but went back to cleaning his fingernails.

"What about the Ferris wheel and food trucks?" The question came from Jezzie. "Are you handling that okay?"

Kimi gave a brisk nod. "I only have five trucks confirmed. I need to line up five more, but my brother's giving me a lead on that. I'm sure I'll be able to get them all scheduled. The guy who does the Ferris wheel is dragging his feet about confirming. I'm going to give him another call tomorrow and then will start to look elsewhere if he's not willing to sign on the dotted line yet."

"Would you like me to call him for you?" Huh. Kimi hadn't expected Owen to offer anything, but... "You have a lot on your plate with the festival, not to mention school and work. I could fit in a call to him."

Kimi glanced down at her phone and skimmed her notes again before looking up. "That would be a huge help. I'm either on the job or in school when he's available, and he's always at work when I have time to talk. I think that's part of the reason we haven't ironed things out yet."

Owen tapped something into his own phone. "Give me his contact info, and I'll call him as soon as it's a decent hour tomorrow."

The meeting let out a few minutes after that. Owen loitered by the door as Kimi turned all the lights off. "Would you like to get a bite to eat?"

She would have loved to. Despite the sometimes abrupt way he spoke, Owen was a genuinely nice guy, and she liked the way he made her feel. Her insides warmed up whenever he was near, and something about the way he treated her gave her a sense of empowerment. He didn't treat her art therapy degree like a whim or a risky venture the way some of her friends and family first had. He talked about it and her future plans as though they were certain, like he believed she could accomplish anything she wanted. "I can't tonight, sorry. I have a test tomorrow, and I'm not quite ready for it. I'll be spending the night with a pot of coffee and all my class notes."

"Then I'll see you tomorrow. Monday."

He made it sound important, but she couldn't place why. "Monday matters because...?"

A grin lit his face. "Remember? I've decided to try a new coffee drink every Monday. So think of a good one to surprise me with. Although I don't think you can top that dulce de leche bon bon."

Kimi chuckled. "Monday. How could I forget? When I get bored with studying tonight and need to clear my head, that's what I'll work on — finding the perfect new drink for Dr. Owen Pratt."

Fourteen

Owen rounded the corner to Kimi's kiosk, but Kimi was absent. A man stood in her place. "Where's Kimi?"

The man in the kiosk glanced at his watch and smiled. "You must be Owen. She said 7:05 on the dot."

"Where's Kimi?"

The man — Toshihiro according to his nametag — reached for an empty cup. "Kimiko is out sick. She told me that I should put together a triple shot half-caff Mexican mocha, though, when you arrived."

"I spent time with her last night. She wasn't ill."

One of Toshihiro's eyebrows inched up. "My baby sister is getting a little old for all-nighters. Drank too much coffee and ate too much chocolate to get through her study session. Said she woke up this morning and felt like her insides were trying to claw their way out of her body. So I'm covering her shift. That way she can rest before she takes her test. Apparently it's an important one."

Owen didn't like the description of Kimi's pain or the flippant way Toshihiro delivered the news. "You're Kimi's brother. That means you own..."

"Sh, don't tell anyone. I kind of like the anonymity. Anybody finds out I'm here, and somebody from food services or some other hospital bureaucracy will want to talk to me about renegotiating my contract, adding another kiosk, redesigning the menu, or something like that. I like it better when I can be the anonymous coffee guy."

"But you fill in for Kimi whenever she needs you to."

He shrugged. "She's family. Besides, being stuck over here by the surgical waiting room means I won't serve anyone who actually works for the hospital. Except for you, of course."

Owen didn't bother to correct Kimi's brother about his employer. Instead, he asked a question that had been nagging at him the past few weeks. "Kimi's earnings include her tips. She probably doesn't get many tips over here, though. People under stress aren't usually in generous moods. Wouldn't you want your sister to have one of the more lucrative spots?"

Toshihiro waggled his head back and forth. "She was right. You're smart. The surgical waiting room is a tough spot. People who are over here can be stressed out, at the end of their rope. You never know from one day to the next what you'll be dealing with here, and Kimi has the personality to handle that. She loves people, and she's naturally cheerful. Putting her in this part of the hospital was a strategic choice. If it helps, though, I do pay her a bit more for taking this spot."

Owen swept his gaze over the waiting room. Palpable worry lined people's faces. "Placing Kimi here was a good decision." Toshihiro didn't need to know that his reasons for thinking so were mostly selfish.

Owen shut down his computer. The day had been a long one, and he was ready to get home, eat some leftover lasagna, and play some online chess. As he locked his door, though, his plans changed.

"Dr. Pratt, report to the ER, please. Dr. Pratt, report to the ER."

He was pretty sure he was the only Dr. Pratt on site, but why would anyone page him to the Emergency Room?

Ten minutes later, Owen pushed through the back doors into the ER and approached the reception desk. "I believe I was paged."

The woman glanced up. "Name?"

"Dr. Pratt. It went out over the hospital intercom."

She nodded and pointed to her left. "Cubicle C10."

He turned on his heel and headed straight for the designated cubicle. Could it be one of his kids? Was it another blood sugar anomaly? They would have been sent to PICU, though, not stuffed into a corner of the ER. He'd have gotten an alert on his phone, too, if any of his clinical trial kids had been admitted. Still...

Owen hurried down the corridor and swept the curtain aside when he came to C10.

"Thank goodness. I was afraid you'd already left for the day."

"Kimi? What are you doing here?"

She whimpered and clutched her stomach. "Acute appendicitis."

He dropped into the chair by her bed. "Has it ruptured?"

"No." Sweat beaded her brow. "But it feels like someone's skewering me with a red-hot fireplace poker. And I couldn't find my phone to call anyone. Paging you was my last hope."

Without thinking, he took her hand and started praying. "Lord, I ask you to comfort Kimi, be with the doctors and staff, and see to her needs. Help her family not to worry and show me how I can best be of service. In Jesus' name, Amen."

She clutched his hand. "I'm so glad you were here."

The nurse bustled into the cubicle, interrupting the moment. "We're about to wheel you in for surgery, sweetheart. Is there anything else you need to tell your gentleman here?"

Kimi squeezed his hand even tighter. "My family. Can you let them know?"

"Of course. Don't you worry about a thing. I'll contact them for you."

Kimi was gone from the room before Owen thought to ask her how exactly he was supposed to reach them. He phoned the church, but it was well after hours, and as expected, his call went straight to voice mail. He thought briefly of Senator Yamada, but he wasn't sure the senator would know how to get ahold of Kimi's family, and in any event, Owen lacked the prestige to be able to reach the senator after hours.

Aha! Makayla.

A quick scroll through his contacts list gave him the Maskeys' phone number. He punched Call and tapped his fingers on his knee as it rang.

"Hello?"

"Angela, this is Dr. Pratt."

"It's late. Is everything okay?" Panic laced her words, and Owen kicked himself. He should have started by saying it had nothing to do with Makayla. That would always be their first assumption whenever he called.

"It's Kimi. She's been admitted to the hospital, but she lost her phone. She asked me to notify her family, but I have no way to reach them. I wondered if you'd ever met any of them or knew how I could get a hold of them."

"Um, hold on. I think I have her mom's contact info. We met at an art showing where Kimi had some paintings on display..."

Art showing? Owen had been under the impression that Kimi's art was limited to caricatures and sketches for tourists.

"Yes, here it is. Kayoko Fairchild." Angela rattled off the phone number, and Owen jotted it down on a notepad.

"Thank you."

"Is there anything we can do?"

Owen shook his head before he remembered she couldn't see him. "I don't think so. Just keep her in prayer. I'm sure she'll appreciate it."

"Of course."

Angela disconnected the call with a goodbye, and Owen frowned at the hand-written number. He hadn't mentioned Kimi's surgery. Even though he'd been in the ER in the capacity of friend, the HIPAA laws were too ingrained in him. He couldn't reveal patient information without written permission.

Reality sank in. Those same HIPAA laws would affect whether or not Owen could inform Kimi's family about anything. He dashed over to the front desk to pull up her file and take a look at her paperwork.

A few minutes later, he sighed with relief. She had listed three people the hospital could share information with. Her mother, her brother, and a Michael Fairchild, presumably her father. She's scrawled a note across the column for contact information. *Will have to add #s later.*

Owen punched in the number Angela Maskey had given him and held his phone to his ear.

"Hello?"

"Is this Mrs. Fairchild?"

"Who is this?"

"My name is Dr. Owen Pratt. I'm calling for..." He glanced at the note he'd scribbled. "I'm calling for Mrs. Kayoko Fairchild."

"This is she. What can I do for you?"

"Kimi asked me to get in touch with you. She's been admitted to Ferito Technology Memorial Hospital with acute appendicitis. They've taken her in for surgery."

"Surgery? Kimiko? Why didn't she call us?"

"I'm honestly not sure. Either she lost her phone or it died. She only reached me because she had them page the entire hospital for me. I got to the ER just before they wheeled her in to surgery, and she asked me to notify you."

A man came on the phone then. "What part of the hospital do we come to?"

"The surgical waiting room. There's a parking garage labeled specifically for surgery. That's the one you want. From there, cross the street and head to the nearest major entrance you see. The receptionist can direct you. I'll be in the waiting room as well in case there's any news." He wasn't listed on the HIPAA form, though, so the surgeon shouldn't tell him anything. He might as a professional courtesy, but Owen didn't see any reason to explain all that.

"All right, we're on our way. And what's your name?"

"Owen Pratt. Dr. Owen Pratt."

"Okay, Dr. Pratt. We'll see you as soon as we can."

The line went dead, and Owen slipped out of the ER and made his way toward the surgical waiting room. That corner of the hospital wouldn't be the same without Kimi bustling around her kiosk. A quick glance at his watch told him it was well past the hour for coffee anyway.

Sure enough, the kiosk stood in shadow.

Owen walked over to one of the low-slung chairs and sat.

He had every confidence in the hospital's staff and Kimi's surgical team. Why, then, was his stomach in a jumble?

FIFTEEN

Strange sounds echoed around Kimi. Was she in a tunnel? That's what it sounded like.

She concentrated and tried to block out the beeping and focus on voices, but the words were too soft.

"Kimiko? Are you awake? Open your eyes."

Ah, Mom was there. She would take care of everything.

Kimi forced her eyes open. "Hi Mom. Dad."

Her father took her hand. "You gave us quite a scare, young lady. Did you know it was appendicitis when you called in sick?"

She rolled her eyes. "Art therapy, Dad. Totally not the same thing as a medical degree."

His eyes crinkled at the corner. "Good to see you're feeling like yourself."

Mom leaned in close and straightened Kimi's bedding. "So, dear, we met your young man."

Kimi tried to sit up, but the pain in her abdomen compelled her back to the pillows. "I don't have a man, young or otherwise."

She looked to her dad for help, but he sank into one of the room's two chairs and shrugged. She was on her own.

113

"He seems nice. Knowledgeable, too. He's a doctor, you know."

Kimi attempted a deep breath, but her post-op pain made that nearly impossible. She settled for a shallow one instead. "The next time one of you has excruciating abdominal pain, you should call him. He'd probably be able to tell you whether it's appendicitis or just too much caffeine and sushi."

Her mother tsked. "You're not getting any younger, dear. You shouldn't make light of this."

Kimi grabbed her mother's hand, which still flitted about and fidgeted with her bedding. "Mom. You said you'd lay off, remember? That you were glad to let me live my life the way I chose. And you already have three grandkids, so it's not like I need to be in a hurry to bring anymore Fairchilds into the world."

Her mother offered a soft smile. "He stayed until the surgeon came out and told us you were in Recovery. He didn't want to impose by coming back to your room, but he waited with us through your whole surgery. That means something, doesn't it? Or am I not up to date on what passes for romance these days? Does it only count if he tweets that he's at the hospital or updates his relationship status?"

Kimi's head sank back into the pillow. He'd stayed. Could her mother be right? Did that mean something? The glow heating up her insides told her it did, but this was Owen. Emotions didn't always factor into his decisions.

Her dad stood and pulled her mom close to his side. "I'm taking your mother home so she can sleep. They were able to go in through your belly button or something like that. Normally they'd release you the same day, but apparently your doctor friend persuaded them to keep you overnight. We'll be by to pick you up around ten in the morning."

Kimi rested a hand on her abdomen. "Did anyone tell Toshihiro? I won't be in to work for a few days."

"Give me some credit, Kimiko. I may not know the difference between a therapist and a doctor, but I know the importance of coffee in a hospital. I called your brother first thing. He said to take as long as you need but to touch base by the weekend so he can plan next week's schedule."

"Your parents are different from what I expected." Owen sat in a chair in the Fairchild's living room and watched her with eagle-eyed precision.

"How so?" It was Thursday afternoon, and Owen had phoned her parents to ask if it was okay for him to stop by for a visit. Her mother had, of course, said absolutely.

"They're part of the mystery of Kimi Fairchild, the girl who lots of other people called

Kimiko even though that wasn't the name on her official coffee kiosk nametag."

She chuckled and winced.

"Sorry."

"For what?" There he went confusing her again.

"I wasn't trying to make you laugh."

Of course not. Did he ever intentionally say anything funny? "My grandma came over from Japan as a child. She grew up and married an Irish-American. She wanted her kids to be American, too, but she also wanted them to remember their Japanese heritage. So she gave them each a traditional first name. Mom grew up and married my blond-haired, blue-eyed dad. She's never thought of us as anything but American, but she honored her mother's wishes regarding our first names."

"Just your first names?"

Kimi nodded.

"What's your middle name?"

She winced. "Anabelle."

"You don't like it?" His eyebrows rose with his question.

"I don't dislike it, I guess. I don't really claim it, either, though." She was content to be Kimi Fairchild. She didn't need more.

Mom came into the room and set a traditional tea service on the coffee table. "May I pour you some tea, Dr. Pratt?"

116

"Of course, but please call me Owen."

Kimi swallowed a groan. Her mother was determined to see her paired off. The sinking feeling in the pit of her stomach was noticeably absent this time, though. That couldn't mean what she thought it meant, could it?

Maybe it was time to cut back on the pain meds.

Once her mother left the room, Owen took a long draw on his tea. "It's good, but not quite what I expected."

"How so?"

"I guess I thought it would be a bit more exotic."

Kimi smirked. "Don't let her fool you. My mom uses a traditional Japanese service, but I'm sure she bought the tea on sale at the local grocery store."

"So how are you feeling?" His words were casual, but he watched her with a physician's eyes.

"Better. The doctor said I could resume normal activity in three or four days, but then I told him my normal activity involves standing on my feet for hours at a time."

"What did he say to that?"

She chuckled. "That I shouldn't be surprised if it takes me a week to get back on my feet. I figure I'll be back at work on Monday."

Owen tapped his fingers against his knee. "Will we still have a committee meeting on Sunday?"

Kimi nodded. "I should be fine to attend church Saturday night and run the meeting Sunday evening."

Owen frowned. "Will you be all right to drive yourself? I can give you a ride if you'd like. To both."

Kimi glanced over Owen's shoulder and saw her mother hovering in the hallway. Then her mom gave her a double thumbs-up. Kimi's groan brought Owen to his feet.

"Are you all right? Should I get your mom?"

Kimi held up a hand. "I'm fine. I just thought of something that made me groan. I think I'll be okay to drive by the weekend, but since I'd rather not overtire myself, I would appreciate a ride if it's not too much trouble. And if you can tolerate our loud Saturday music again."

His eyes crinkled at the corners. "The company makes the music worth it."

Sixteen

Owen picked Kimi up for their Sunday committee meeting. Church the night before had been much like the last time he'd gone, too-loud music and a spot-on sermon. He could compromise on the one as long as he wasn't asked to on the other.

They drove along in silence for the first little bit before Kimi spoke up. "Did you talk to the guy about the Ferris wheel?"

"I did. He's not ready to commit."

"He's worked our Fall Festival every year since the church started it." She frowned. "Until I took the event over three years ago. He became less amenable then."

"Why?"

"I have three strikes against me. I'm part-Japanese, short, and female. Which do you think he objects to? Or maybe he has something against artists and coffee-drinkers."

None of those was a good answer. "We need a larger sampling of festival organizers before we can begin testing any of your theories."

"Does everything boil down to science?" Kimi's laughter teased his senses just enough to make him want to hear more of it.

"Like atoms and molecules, people usually behave in predictable patterns when submitted to the same stimuli. There are more variables with people, but yes, I tend to process at most situations in terms of the scientific method."

"Does this scientific method of yours leave room for feelings?"

"Feelings?" Was the air conditioner working? The car was getting awfully hot and stuffy.

"Yeah. Love, anger, or anything like that."

"Of course. God made us in His image, and He is capable of both great love and great anger. It makes sense for people to have those feelings, too."

"But...?"

Owen resisted the urge to tug at his collar. "Emotions are difficult to quantify. They're not just variables. They're messy variables."

"Do you ever let your feelings dictate your actions, or do you always rely on logic?"

"Where are these questions coming from?" He beat a *tat-a-tat* rhythm out on the steering wheel.

"I want to understand you better."

People didn't usually make that kind of effort with him. "Logic is always going to be my fallback position, but emotions can certainly override logic."

"Give me an example. Tell me about a time when you allowed your feelings to take over and put logic in its place."

He glanced her way. Her eyes were clear, and her skin tone normal. No obvious sign of fever or delirium. "Logic's place should be front and center."

"Fine, fine. Tell me about a time when you let emotion take over and put logic out of its place."

"Last night. I went to a contemporary church service on a Saturday night. That wasn't because of logic."

A soft smile shaped her mouth. "Hm. Well, I'm glad emotion won that one."

As Owen pulled into the church's parking lot, Kimi cleared her throat. "I'd like to ask you a question, but it's the sort of question that, if misunderstood, could hurt somebody's feelings."

Talk about cryptic. "Okay."

"Um, I'm not going to ask now."

"You're not making sense. You might as well ask me."

"I'll ask after our meeting tonight. Your answer might be long or I might upset you, and I'd rather not do that before we go into the meeting."

"Then why not wait till afterward to say anything at all?"

"Because that would have been logical...?"

She had to be talking in riddles. That was the only reasonable explanation.

Kimi opened her door and pulled herself up out of the car. "Logic isn't the thing on my mind."

"Then, what is on your mind?" He held his exasperation in check. Barely.

"You. My question. Second-guessing myself and wondering if I should ask it or leave it alone."

She'd never struck him as the indecisive type. "When you want to know something, the best way to get an answer is to ask."

"Yeah, that's kind of what I figured, but if I put the question off, I might talk myself out of asking."

"So instead you told me you would ask me later?"

She stepped through as he opened the front door of the church for her. "It makes sense to me. Doesn't it make sense to you?"

He shook his head. "Some people have personalized ring tones. You took logic and personalized it the same way. I wouldn't have believed that was possible before now."

"Is that bad?"

Yes. But then — no. "If I plan to analyze it further, it'll need a name. What do you think of Logic Without Equal?"

A soft jab to his solar plexus made her opinion clear. "You're not making fun of my name, are you?"

He held up both hands. "Never. Wouldn't dream of it."

Owen watched Kimi throughout the meeting. Quite the opposite of her normal behavior, she remained seated the entire time, and he found himself questioning whether or not she was ready to return to work the next day. She didn't look like she would welcome a full day of standing on her feet and serving coffee.

Bill talked about the small bump he'd seen in volunteer sign-ups and how many more Sunday School classes he planned to visit over the coming weeks.

Jezzie pulled out her notebook when her turn came. "Our music group situation is still in flux, but I stopped by Worship Practice this morning and let everyone know how I'd overbooked by accident and wouldn't have their final schedule until early October. They were all gracious. I was worried somebody's feelings would be hurt, but I should have known better. God's got my back even when I forget how much He cares."

Kimi tipped her head in June's direction next, and the young teacher took her cue. "I sent you all the information you requested, but I've been playing with the floor plan we set up, and I think I have a solution." She passed some papers around the table. "Most of the booths can afford to give up five inches of space. That'll allow two of them to fit into our existing row. I found this other little corner, though, that's not getting much use in the current plan. What if I put all the preschool-appropriate games there? That way we're not reorganizing because I overbooked. We're reorganizing so that visitors can maximize their enjoyment."

Bill snorted. "I don't hate the idea, but I'm not a big fan of spin. Just say it like it is."

Owen had to agree with the older man, but he saw no purpose in repeating what had already been said.

Kimi studied the map June had passed around. "Let me sleep on it. If everyone's in agreement, I'll forward this on to the fire marshal's office this week so they have time to sign off on it. I want to study it one more time with fresh eyes first, though, and make sure I'm not overlooking anything obvious."

"Sounds like a plan to me." Jezzie folded her papers and stuffed them into her purse.

Bill grumbled his assent.

June nodded enthusiastically.

"Good. Now, as you know, I ended up in the hospital Monday night, so I haven't accomplished much on the food truck front, but Owen has some news about the Ferris wheel."

All eyes turned to Owen, and even though he'd stood before thesis committees, he felt his palms dampen. "Mr. Martins doesn't want to commit yet for the Fall Festival. He says he'll know in two weeks. He could be holding out for a better offer. I'm not sure. If he's not willing to put the festival on his calendar yet, perhaps we should start looking elsewhere for a Ferris wheel."

Bill responded first. "I don't have patience for dilly-dallying. I say find someone else."

Jezzie nodded, but June disagreed. "We've been using the same person all these years. To dump him and run seems kind of harsh."

Kimi glanced around the table before answering the unspoken query. "Make some calls. Find out what it'll cost and if anybody else is even still available. Don't make any commitments. We can talk about it again next week."

Everyone filed out of the room, and Owen held the door for Kimi to exit.

Once they were settled back in his car, seatbelts dutifully clicked into place, Owen braced himself. Kimi's audibly deep breath did little to alleviate his irrational fear over her impending discussion. Every embarrassing question he'd ever been asked in college came back to him.

"Are you on the autism spectrum?"

Of all the things he'd anticipated, that wasn't anywhere on the list. "Would it matter if I was?"

"No, not really. I just wondered. I've known a few people on the spectrum, and sometimes you remind me of them. But sometimes you don't."

"Ah, I see. It's my charming good looks and witty personality that makes you ask, isn't it?"

Kimi chuckled. "Here I was worried the question might upset you, and instead you're being Mr. Funny."

Owen eased onto the freeway before answering. "When I was young, my mom took me in to get tested. The doctor put me through a whole panel of tests."

"What conclusion did he reach?"

He cast a sideways glance at her. "In the end, he decided I was a sociopath."

Seventeen

Kimi closed her hung-open mouth with enough force to rattle her teeth.

Sociopath?

"How, um, did your mom handle that?"

Owen's smile came easily. "She took me out for ice cream. When I asked about the proper temperature to keep ice cream frozen without causing crystallization, Mom asked the server behind the counter for their training manual so she could answer my questions."

Kimi released the breath she hadn't realized she was holding. "She sounds like a great lady."

"She is. The best, really. My dad, too. God knew I wouldn't grow up to be a C-student with a middle-management job. I'm thankful every day that He gave me to parents who would love me even when they didn't understand me. Um, and maybe I should tell you now that I was joking when I said the doctor told my mom I was a sociopath."

Kimi whipped her head around to stare at Owen. "Two jokes in the last hour?" He was full of surprises. "But for the record, sociopathy isn't something people generally joke about."

A blush climbed his cheeks and Kimi sighed.

"Sorry. That came out sharper than I meant. So what exactly did the doctor tell your mom?"

Owen adjusted the rearview mirror before answering. "He said I was borderline autistic. Some of my test results indicated I might fall somewhere on the spectrum, but others put me nowhere near it. He told her to bring me back in a few years to be tested again if she was still concerned. His advice in the meantime, though, was to let me be myself and explore the world around me as much as I wanted to."

"Ah, so that's when she took you out for ice cream and got the training manual."

"Pretty much. Mom dove in with both feet. Anytime I asked a question, she helped me find the answer. The older I got, the more she didn't even understand the questions I asked, but she made sure I had the right tools to help me search out my answers."

"Did you ever go back to get retested?"

Owen shook his head. "My folks never saw the point, and neither did I. Had I been unhappy or miserable or unable to form relationships with others, then yes, it would have been prudent. As it was, though, I loved my parents, enjoyed my life, and was able to make friends at church."

"I can't quite picture you playing T-ball with the other kids."

"Nah. I talked theology with the pastor and technology with the guy who made microchips and business with the woman who was president of a Fortune 500 company. My friends were usually over the age of forty, but they were still my friends."

"And now?"

"Now that I'm approaching the four-decade mark, I find myself in a unique position. I have spent so much time as an adult pursuing knowledge that I didn't invest enough in developing relationships. My work is important, and my relationships are good. I just..." His voice faded away.

"You can't leave me wondering."

He pulled his car into the driveway at her parents' house. "I'm beginning to wonder if God has someone for me. A serious relationship more-than-friends kind of someone."

Even in the dimness of the car's interior, the blue in his eyes shone bright. They held an invitation that Kimi didn't know how to answer.

"So now it's my turn to ask a question." His words rested in the space between them.

She swallowed, remembering how invasive her own question had been.

"If I asked you out on a date, a proper date that's not for business or related to church, what would you say?"

Her gaze dropped from his blue eyes to his lips. "Are you asking me out?"

Owen shook his head. "Not yet. I don't want the Fall Festival to become awkward if you say no or if we try and it doesn't work out."

There was that stellar logic of his again.

"I am planning to ask you out sometime after the festival."

"Well then, I think it's only proper that a man not receive an answer if he's not asking a question."

Owen's brow drew together. "I did ask a question."

Kimi nodded at him. "Ah, but not the right one."

"Is this Kimi logic again?" He let her off the hook.

"Indubitably." A girl shouldn't give away all her secrets. Besides, she would need time to figure this one out.

Kimi closed the front door and tiptoed toward the stairs. She needed to get some sleep before work in the morning. Her brother planned to hover, and he would report everything back to her parents.

"How was your meeting?" Her dad's voice reached her from the living room, and Kimi changed direction.

"We still have a few kinks to iron out, but I think it'll be a fantastic festival."

He nodded and put aside the book he'd been reading. "It was nice of Owen to give you a ride."

"He's a nice guy."

"Is that all he is to you? A nice guy?"

Neither of her parents was good at dancing around a subject. She loved that about them, but she wasn't ready for this discussion. "Do we need to do this right now?"

He picked his book up again, thumbed through it, and set it back down. "I think we do. You've never been inclined to settle down, and that's always been okay with me. I want you to live the life God has for you. Something about Owen, though..." He sighed. "I think he cares for you more than he's saying, and I know you, Kimiko. You don't want to be responsible for hurting him."

Kimi sat down on the edge of the sage green couch. "He said he doesn't want to complicate anything while we're still working on the Fall Festival together but that he plans to ask me out on a date once it's over."

Dad nodded. "And have you decided yet how you'll answer him when the time comes?"

She shook her head. "He's a nice guy."

"But?"

"But he's different, you know? A lot different."

"Different isn't a four-letter word. It doesn't have to be bad. In fact, if I recall, there was a time when you prided yourself on your many differences."

Kimi picked at a nail. Did her dad know how to hit the mark or what? "Remember the missionary who came to our church when I was a senior in high school? He talked about how important it was for people to count the cost prior to entering the mission field. Too many people didn't realize what they were getting into, and they dove into mission work only to get disillusioned to the point of walking away and never looking back. He said that if people counted the cost and understood how hard it would be before they started, they would stay longer and do more."

Dad's chin tipped down. "I can't put a face to it, but the memory's there. So is that what you're doing — counting the cost?"

Kimi switched to a different nail. "I think Owen is someone who could love deeply but who is never going to get caught up in romance. Do I want to date someone who loves me but never says it? Or shows it?"

"Do you honestly think he'd never express it?"

She shrugged. "I'm not sure, but I have to ask the question, you know? I need to count the cost. If that's the way it would be, is it worth pursuing?"

"That's all that's bothering you?" Dad knew her too well.

"Not entirely."

He waited, his eyebrows barely lifting.

"Owen has this incredible mind. Lives are being saved because of his single-minded focus. It's like he walks in this perfectly straight line, and I twirl around in circles."

Her dad's eyes warmed. "Circles can be fun. Remember when you wanted me to teach you to dance?"

How could she forget? "I was eight, and I insisted we not move any of the furniture out of the way so we could dance in loop-de-loops around everything."

"Those loop-de-loops are some of my fondest memories."

Pressure built behind Kimi's eyes. "But what if getting involved with me changes him? What if he's the man who might cure cancer someday, but dancing loop-de-loops with me makes him too emotional and he loses that part of himself that gives him the ability to solve impossible puzzles and save lives?" She hadn't realized how much that worry weighed on her until the words had come flooding out of her.

Dad stared, this time with his eyebrows drawn together. "How old are you now? Thirty?"

He was hopeless. "Thirty-three."

"Whatever." He waved his hand. "The point is, you're an adult. You are capable of making your own choices. I trust you to make a wise one, and I trust you to keep Owen's feelings — which are clearly already involved — in mind as you make it. I've watched you grow into this woman who astounds me. You have a creative and carefree spirit, but you care deeply for people and often base your own personal decisions on what's best for other people. I can't tell you whether or not Owen's the one God has for you, but I can tell you with certainty that if he's not, you will find the best possible way to let him know that."

Her anxiety began to seep away. "Thank you. That means a lot."

He wasn't quite ready to give up his role as parental advisor. "As you make this decision, though, I encourage you to seek counsel from someone far wiser than your dear old Dad. Hm?"

Kimi rose from the couch and started back toward the stairs. Then she turned around, approached her father, and planted a kiss on his forehead. "Thanks, Dad. Goodnight."

"Anytime, sweetheart. Go get some good rest. I'll be praying for you and Owen. Oh..."

She paused.

"Don't get annoyed at your brother tomorrow. Your mother called him at least ten times today to make sure he's not going to leave you on your own. He might be a little haggard by the time you see him."

Kimi shook her head as she climbed the stairs, one hand tightly gripping the rail. Even though they hadn't bothered her in a couple of days, she kept expecting the stitches to pull.

As for her dad, he was right. She needed to seek wisdom from a higher source.

God, are you listening? Of course you are. There's this guy, see...

EIGHTEEN

Owen was on his way to get his morning coffee when his phone rang. He usually returned calls after he got back to his office. A glance at the screen told him this one was important, though.

"Dr. Jameson, what can I do for you?"

"Have you been avoiding me?" His mentor's voice was pitched higher than usual.

Owen couldn't blame him for being confused. Avoidance wasn't his typical modus operandi. "I've been busy. There's a difference."

Dr. Jameson chuckled. "I'll give you the benefit of the doubt. I wanted to let you know our New Drug Application is under review. My source at the FDA tells me someone from HELP requested a copy of the application as well. Should I be worried?"

Owen could only think of one person. "Senator Yamada?"

"If I had to guess, yes."

"He said the committee doesn't see the NDA unless they specifically request it."

"Is there anything I should know about?"

"We had a cordial conversation, and he strikes me as a fair man. If he finds a problem with the NDA, I think he'd say so and not try to bog it down in committee. He has more important things to spend his time on, don't you think?"

Dr. Jameson lacked his usual jaunty confidence. "That's what I'd like to think, too, but he knew the girl you were with. Has anything happened there? A lover scorned or anything like that?"

Owen pulled the phone away from his ear and stared at it for a second before returning it to its place. "She's not my lover, and I'm pretty sure I haven't scorned her. Is that even an appropriate question?"

Dr. Jameson sighed like a little old lady asked to babysit sugared-up three-year-old triplets. "Appropriate? Probably not. Necessary? Yes. Drugs have been derailed for lesser reasons before. I just need to make sure there aren't any messes to clean up."

"What do you expect me to do? I would prefer to wait and see what happens with the NDA. Borrowing trouble won't help anyone."

"All right. We'll take the wait-and-see approach. You understand, don't you, that I had to ask about the girl?"

Owen gritted his teeth. "There was never any reason to ask about her, but I see why you feel compelled to make my personal life your business."

"I guess that'll have to do." Dr. Jameson's voice softened. "The conversation up to now has been between you and me. As long as we don't hit a glitch with the NDA, it won't be brought up before the board. The answer to this next question, though, is one I take back to them."

Dr. Jameson paused, and the silence stretched between them until Owen finally broke it. "Very well."

"Have you given any thought to what you'd like to work on once this is wrapped up?"

Something was different about the kiosk. Owen could see Kimi, but...

He approached, carefully stepping over the cable that ran along the floor while trying to figure out what had changed. As soon as Kimi spotted him, she smiled. "Hey there. You never told me what you thought of the Mexican mocha. Did you like it?"

"It was good, but not as good as the dulce de leche bon bon. Are you sitting down?"

Kimi popped to her feet. "My sweet brother didn't want me to be on my feet all day, so he got me a stool to sit on."

"That was nice of him."

"He's also stopped by pretty much every twenty minutes to check and make sure I'm okay. Because he texted once, but I was with a customer and took too long to get back to him. So now he's coming in person."

"I like your brother."

Kimi grinned. "Yeah, me too. But don't tell him I said so."

"Do you have a coffee recommendation for me?"

"I do." Kimi got to work with the espresso machine, and Owen left her to it. When she was done, she handed him the cup. "Give it a try."

He took a careful sip. "Oh... I like that." He took a healthier-sized drink. "A lot. What is it?"

"That is my house special Chai Latte."

He took another drink. "So not a standard drink?"

"Sort of, but with my own little twist."

"You're spoiling me. No other barista will ever compare."

Laughter moved along the edges of her smile. "Took you long enough to catch onto my secret plan."

"I'm the only person in line. Why don't you join me for a drink?"

Kimi held up her steaming cup. "Already ahead of you. Normally I wouldn't because bathroom breaks are few and far between, but with my brother stalking me today, I figured I could splurge. He can stand in for me if I need a minute to run to the lady's room."

"Well..." Owen tipped his cup toward hers. "...Cheers."

She took a sip of her drink before spearing him with her eyes. "So, is this a date then? Because it sounds like you just asked me out for coffee..."

The question hung there draped in all its caffeinated glory. "Um." Owen cleared his throat. "We'll call this an informal date. After all, I didn't even pay for your drink or hold the door open for you. I'm pretty sure that makes it less than an actual date."

"The door's a technicality, but I'll give you points on the paying-for-it part." Kimi winked as she said the last, and Owen stared.

What was it about her? She made him want to be somehow more. When he was around her, he wanted to be the man who made her laugh and smile and... wink. He'd never cared whether or not he was that guy to any woman before, but with Kimi... Everything was different with her.

Owen swirled the drink in his cup. "You do serious art, too. Not just caricatures."

Her forehead wrinkled. "What constitutes serious art? I'll have you know I take my caricatures quite seriously."

He shook his head. "You led me to believe your artwork consisted of drawings tourists and that sort of thing, but Mrs. Maskey mentioned a showing. It surprised me."

Her eyes widened. "Oh. I'd forgotten she went to that one." She offered a half-shrug. "They're not exclusive showings or anything. I know a guy who runs a gallery, and every now and then, he likes to showcase local artists and invites me to participate. Sometimes he likes what I bring him. Sometimes he doesn't."

"Still, that's quite an honor. Is it presumptuous to ask how much your work sells for?" Did she do paintings, sculptures, or something else entirely?

Color stained her cheeks as she studied the teabags to her left. "Working for my brother pays my rent and other bills. My art pays for college."

Wow. She might not be selling items for millions of dollars, but if her art earned her enough to pay for college... He'd allowed the description of her bohemian lifestyle to sway his opinion of her artistic talent, and he'd underestimated her as a result. "I don't suppose you'd give me the name of the gallery?"

She shook her head. "No, but if I still like you the next time I have a showing, I'll make sure you get an invitation."

Another customer stepped into line, and Owen reluctantly moved aside. "I look forward to it. I'll talk to you later."

Kimi turned her attention to the waiting nurse, clearly oblivious to the maelstrom of emotion churning inside him.

"Lily! Back from your honeymoon?" She spared him one last glance, and her fingers waggled in a uniquely Kimi wave — delicate, feminine, funny, and powerful.

How could such a small motion capture the essence of a person? And how could a woman be made up of so many contradictory components?

"Peach tea with lemon, please." The nurse — Lily apparently — leaned on the counter. "I wanted to come by and say thank you for the wedding gift. It was beautiful."

"You're welcome. I enjoyed making it. So... Looks like your guy got the Republican nomination."

The nurse chuckled. "He's not my guy."

Kimi's voice followed him. "Hm. Everyone knows Jefferson David Taylor was your patient after he got shot..."

Owen forced himself to concentrate on his feet and where he landed them. Kimi was too distracting by far, and he wanted the coffee to still be in its cup by the time he made it back to his office.

NINETEEN

Toshihiro approached her kiosk. "Been busy? How you feeling?"

Kimi winked at her brother. "Took you long enough. I thought you forgot about me."

"Huh?"

"You were coming by every twenty minutes, then all of a sudden nothing."

A blush climbed Toshihiro's neck. "I stopped by, but you were having coffee with your friend, so I left you two alone."

Kimi shook her head. "There was no need for that."

He mumbled something.

"What was that?"

"I said, 'not according to Mom.'"

Kimi's stomach flopped. "What has Mom been telling you?"

"Something about a biological clock, seeing you settled down before she dies, and Owen being a doctor."

"She's really going overboard with this, isn't she?"

He chuckled. "I'm just glad you finally have enough of a life for her to think it's worth meddling in. Takes the pressure off me."

"Yeah, but you're happily married with three kids. What's left for her to meddle in?"

He winced. "Uh, hello? Three boys. No granddaughter for Mom. Last week I even caught her talking to Mitch — age eight mind you — about the type of woman he should marry."

"Has she always been a matchmaker? How did I never notice before?" It did seem lately like an alien had taken over her mother's body. A relationship-obsessed alien.

"Ha! She's been matchmaking since I got my first chin whisker. The only reason you didn't realize was because she was focused on me. Eldest son and all that. Then you ran off to Oregon and stayed away."

"Yeah, but I've been back five years now. Has she been trying to matchmake this whole time and I missed it?"

"No way." Toshihiro gave his head a vigorous shake. "You'd have known. A bull moose during mating season is more subtle than Mom."

Kimi winced. "Then why now?"

He gave her a dismissive shrug. "She thought you were looking for an excuse to leave again, so she played it cool. Now that you have a man in your life, though... One of these days, you're going to get home after your classes, and she'll be sitting on your couch reading through bridal magazines. And you won't even know how she got in."

Kimi shuddered. "I don't have a man in my life. You guys are making way too much out of this."

Toshihiro's eyes widened. "Come on Kimi. You're not dumb. You see the way he looks at you."

"I... I don't know how I feel about him."

"He's the first man you haven't dumped after one date since moving back home. So obviously you feel something for him."

"Something, yeah, but I'm not sure it's enough. How do you know if what you feel can sustain a relationship?"

"You don't." Toshihiro tapped his chest. "But you know in here that you *want* it to be enough. That's the key."

"Wanting it and making it happen are two different things."

"Sure, but if you want it to last, then you work at it. You invest the time and energy to make it happen. No relationship is easy, but if you're both committed, then you put in the effort together to make it a good one."

When had her brother grown up and gotten himself filled with sage advice? He even kind of made sense.

Done with work and school for the day, Kimi aimed her car toward the studio apartment she called home. She could almost taste autumn in the snap of the air, but her brother's earlier words distracted her.

Was he right? Was there no way to be sure? Was it more about wanting a relationship to work?

She joked and told people — Owen included — that she was a bohemian at heart. Unconventional, unorthodox, and carefree. In truth, she'd outgrown that a long time ago. It was still a part of her; it just wasn't her identity anymore. At her core, she simply wanted to help people, to make a difference in their lives. She couldn't wait to finish school, pass her boards, and get on with the next chapter in her life.

Did leaving her transient lifestyle behind mean she was ready to settle down in a long-term relationship, though? Until she was certain... The risk was too great. She'd put her parents through a lot of heartache with her escape to the West Coast. She could still hear the shock in her father's voice when she'd told him about the co-op. But she'd loved it there, and she'd thrived. Or at least, she'd thought so at the time. Maybe she'd been wrong about that, too, all this time.

What would Owen say?

She sighed.

He'd probably known since the age of ten exactly what he wanted to do when he grew up. He never would have wandered aimlessly and decided from day to day how to earn a living.

They were so different. Too different.

But... she liked him. More than a little, too. Not just in that hey-let's-be-friends kind of way, either. That factored in, too, didn't it?

Kimi settled into her pew and wondered what Owen was doing. She hadn't needed him to drive her to church this week, so she'd come on her own. She felt his absence, though. Was this what Toshihiro had been talking about?

She crossed her legs and pulled her phone close. As she tapped through to her Bible app, someone squeezed between her and the pew in front of her. It wasn't unusual for people to cross through, but when the person dropped into the seat right beside her, she glanced up.

"Hey." Owen looked at her, one eyebrow lifted.

"Hey."

"Is it okay that I came?"

Of course it was okay. Her angst somehow vanished at the sight of him. A smile even tugged at the corner of her mouth. "Why wouldn't it be?"

"You didn't invite me, so..."

She leaned over and kissed him on the cheek. "Consider that your open invitation." What was she doing? She'd promised herself she wouldn't lead him on, and she was still topsy-turvy where he was concerned. Or not. Maybe she wasn't as confused about her feelings as she thought.

Owen stood as the worship music began, but not before she spotted the silly grin on his face.

Come to think of it, she was pretty sure her grin held a hint of silly, too.

Great. Her one saving grace was that her mother wasn't there to witness what she'd done.

TWENTY

The weeks passed more quickly than Owen could have anticipated. Fall Festival was only a few days away, and everything seemed to have fallen into place. The volunteers were lined up, game booths all set, singing groups satisfied, and food trucks scheduled. Even the Ferris wheel was taken care of, albeit with a new vendor.

On top of that, Owen had been able to spend time with Kimi on a regular basis.

In an effort to make sense of his feelings for her, he'd sat down at one point and tried to make a list of Kimi's attributes. Quantifying his attraction was a sensible thing to do. The problem, however, was that he couldn't boil it down to facts and figures. Her smile made him feel good. She believed the best about people and was fair. She was adventurous, which prevented him from getting too set in his ways. She cared about children and wasn't content to stand on the sidelines and cheer for other people who also cared about them. She was willing to change the whole course of her life so she could be in the trenches working with those kids and helping them herself. Kimi was just about perfect. He even found her overly intrusive mother charming, which, as his father had informed him, meant he had it bad.

He still couldn't figure out, though, if Kimi felt the same way. At times, he was sure of it, but then she would pull back. Reading people had never been his strong suit, but she was by far the most challenging read he'd ever attempted. He couldn't anticipate her next move. He wouldn't be admitting it out loud anytime soon, but that was one of the things that terrified him about her... and one of the things he loved.

Love.

Could it be?

They hadn't known each other very long, but he'd always been able to figure things out quicker than most.

He'd told Kimi he would ask her out on a real date after the festival was over. What if he didn't wait quite that long? What if...?

Owen cringed. The bullhorn added a certain shriek to Kimi's voice that wasn't normally there.

"All right everyone! It's time for the Fall Festival! You all know where you're supposed to be and what you're supposed to be doing, but if you have any questions, you know how to contact me or the person supervising your area. We're going to open the gates in fifteen minutes. Before we do, though, let's pray."

Someone grabbed the bullhorn from her, pushed a couple of buttons, and handed it back. "Lord, thank you for this opportunity to reach out to and touch the lives of people in our community."

Thank goodness. The shriek had vanished.

"Please be with us today as we try to show Your love to the people we come into contact with. Keep everyone safe, and may we glorify You."

Everybody moved away from the gathering and took their places throughout the church's large parking lot and the surrounding acreage.

Kimi waved to him. "Are you ready for this?"

He nodded. "No, probably not."

"I love your certainty."

He couldn't help but grin at her. "Yeah, well, I figure if I can handle Saturday night church then I can handle hordes of screaming children."

"Screaming children who've had too much sugar. Don't forget the sugar. Or the tired, worn-out parents."

"You're not convincing me."

She laughed. "I can be honest now. It's too late for you to back out. So where are you helping?"

"I'm selling tickets for the Ferris wheel this morning and am on trash pick-up duty this afternoon."

"I see Bill put you to work."

"He tried to stick me in a game booth. We cleared that up, though."

Laughter danced in her eyes. "Oh? What'd you tell him?"

"That I'd do anything that didn't require me to make conversation with people."

"You're not as bad at conversation as you think you are."

"Um, yes I am. Obviously I've fooled you, but yes, I'm the world's worst conversationalist."

"Just ask how they're enjoying the weather."

"It's sunny and not too hot. Everyone's enjoying the weather. Next subject?"

"Good point." She bit her bottom lip. "Ticket sales and trash pickup is sounding like a pretty good match right about now."

Owen gave her a quick salute. "And now I'm off to go serve at my station. You did a great job, and today's going to be a rousing success."

The day flew by. The festival was supposed to wrap up at four o'clock. All the equipment needed to be torn down and cleared out before church the next day, and in order for that to go smoothly, daylight was necessary. There was one thing left that Owen wanted to do, though, before everything was powered down for the day.

He caught sight of Kimi and waved to Mr. Sepulveda at the Ferris wheel before jogging after her.

"Hey!"

She turned to him. "Hey yourself. Enjoying the day? I see you didn't run away once the crowd arrived."

He grabbed her hand. "Come on. There's something I want to show you."

Kimi frowned at him. "I'm needed in ten different places right now. I'm not sure I have the time."

"Come on. You want to see this."

She followed when he tugged her hand. Her reluctance didn't bode well for him, but he was already committed to this course of action. It was too late to back out now. Besides, it wasn't in his nature to change direction — or his mind — until he collected enough evidence to prove such a move judicious.

Twenty-One

What had gotten into Owen? He wasn't normally the spontaneous type, yet here he was, dragging her through the thinning crowd on the spur of the moment.

"Get in."

Kimi looked from Owen to the small gate he held open for her. He wanted her to go for a ride on the Ferris wheel? "It takes at least twenty minutes to make the full circuit. I don't have that kind of time."

"Come on. There's nobody else on it right now. I'll have him take us straight up to the top. I just want you to see the fall colors from up there."

She should decline. There was still too much to do. Kimi shielded her eyes as she looked to where the Ferris wheel soared against the skyline, though, and a bubble of excitement began to build in her middle.

It was a Fall Festival after all. The trees would be beautiful from that high up. Kimi capitulated and climbed into the bucket seat. Owen got in after her, and the man running the Ferris wheel closed it, locked it into place, and gave them the safety spiel.

They soon came to a rest at the top, and Owen turned to her. "What do you think?"

The panorama of color took her breath away. Red, gold, and orange stretched as far as the eye could see with the occasional green interspersed. "Wow. I've been so busy planning, I didn't even notice the leaves had changed."

"I thought you'd enjoy it. The artist in you can't help but admire the color."

"You're not an artist, though, and you admire it."

Pink tinged Owen's cheeks. "It's different for me. I appreciate it from a scientific point of view. You appreciate it from a purely visual perspective."

The irony wasn't lost on Kimi. She'd been the one single-minded in her task, and Owen had interrupted to make her stop and simply enjoy something for a minute. He was full of surprises. "Thank you for making me stop long enough to enjoy this."

"An invitation to an art showing appeared in my hospital mail this week."

She glanced his way long enough to notice his more-inscrutable-than-usual expression before returning her attention to the explosion of color around them. "It's not till December. I'm surprised the invitations went out already."

"I look forward to going."

Owen's voice was different. They were sitting down, so he couldn't be winded. Something, though...

"Will you go out with me?"

Her head whipped around. "What?"

"I said I'd ask after the festival, but this was too good an opportunity to pass up. So I'm asking. Will you go out with me?"

Kimi returned her gaze to the trees. "To the showing?"

The smallest shake of his head. "I'd like that, but I didn't plan to wait that long. I hoped we could do something this week. Dinner. Shopping. Or both. You could help me buy a new chair for my office. The last one broke..." His words drifted into silence.

Why were her palms suddenly sweaty? Because she cared. She cared how this went, maybe more than she should at this point in the relationship. "I worry sometimes. That we're so different."

"Hydrogen and oxygen are two completely different elements, but when you mix them together, they become water, something new and unlike either of the original elements."

"Is that what you think we are? Hydrogen and oxygen?"

He shook his head. "We're Kimi and Owen, and I like the way that sounds when I say it in my heart."

A band of warmth squeezed her chest. "Me too."

The Ferris wheel started moving again, and they approached the ground at a leisurely pace. "Is that a yes?"

Kimi rested her hand against his cheek. "It's a yes. I'm not sure this is going to be a straight path for us, but I'd like to travel it with you."

Owen's eyes shone blue in the light of the slowly setting sun. "I've been walking in a straight path my whole life. Until you, I didn't realize there was any other way."

"Walk with me for long, and we'll be doing loop-de-loops that make the hay bale maze look tame."

He cast a puzzled look her way.

"You live life on the straight-and-narrow. You know where you are and where you want to go, and you walk a straight line between the two. I take my time and wander in different directions and circle back on my own tracks."

His eyes lit from within. "We're both going to the same place, though."

"Yeah, but…"

The Ferris wheel came to a stop, and they disembarked. Owen reached behind the ticket counter to pull something out. He handed Kimi a bouquet of red and yellow daisies. "As long as you're with me, we can do all the loop-de-loops you want."

"How…?" She took the flowers. "These are beautiful. How did you know they're my favorite?"

"You may have mentioned it a time or two."

Had she? She didn't remember ever saying anything about flowers. "What if I had said no?"

"Then they would still be under the counter. No point making you feel bad."

Kimi chuckled. Owen was always going to give her an honest answer, no doubt about it.

She buried her nose in the bouquet and took a deep whiff. "They're perfect. Thoughtful. Romantic, even."

"They're supposed to be."

"Why?" And here she'd been, worrying about his ability to be romantic.

Owen reached for her free hand and brought it to his lips. "Because you're worth it."

His kiss against her fingers sent warm tingles racing up her arm and sparks soaring into the sky. A real kiss was sure to be even more potent. She wasn't sure she'd survive.

And just like that, the moment was broken with the ring of Owen's phone. One glance at the screen, and every inch of his demeanor transformed. It had to be a business call. "Yes?... Mm-hm... That's... Yes, of course. Thank you."

He pocketed his phone and turned to her with a face-splitting grin. "The FDA approved our NDA. The drug trial... Makayla... We'll be able to help more children now."

Owen was something else. Different from any other man she'd ever met, certainly. Where other men might care about the fame, the money, or the protocol, his first thought was for the kids whose lives could be saved.

Kimi grabbed his hand and pulled him close, lifted her arms to circle his neck — flowers and all — and tugged his head down toward her. "You're spectacular, you know that?" She'd been worried that he was too different for her, but what if she'd had it backwards? Words started tumbling out of her mouth. "Walking the straight path has gotten you this far in life. I'm not sure... What if I break you?" She rested her forehead against his, each syllable choking her more than the one before. "What if spending more time with me means you lose your way and can't invent new cancer drugs?"

Tears burned the backs of her eyes at the thought of losing him. But what if it was true? What if she was too different? Or what if his feelings for her compromised his ability to analyze and think through the problems and puzzles that could save lives?

Owen's eyes closed. His Adam's apple bobbed as he swallowed. When his eyes opened again, they burned bright. One hand came up to cup her neck, and the other rested on her shoulder. "Stop thinking so much."

His lips touched hers, and all thought fled Kimi's mind. There was no room for worry or logic. Heat built in her middle until it burst in an explosion of color, a painter's palette of every hue lighting up her mind's eye and then settling into a warm glow.

And she knew. In that moment, she knew. This is the life she wanted. Tomorrow, the day after, and the day after that one. Heat and color and kisses... and Owen.

He leaned back, his breathing ragged. "I'd rather walk the loop-de-loops with you than walk the straight path alone." His touch feather light, he stroked a finger across her lips. "Don't put an end to us before we get a chance to start."

Kimi pulled her arms from around his neck, fingered the semi-crushed bouquet of daisies, and stared up at Owen. "We might need to compromise."

He took a step toward her, but she took a matching one back. Then he held up his hands in surrender and frowned at her. "I'm not sure I like the sound of that."

"There will be times when you need all your focus for work. I don't want to distract you from what's important."

He growled deep in his throat. "What do you suggest?"

Kimi took her time, smelled the flowers again, and dug the toe of her shoe into the ground. "Maybe I can walk the straight path with you Monday, Wednesday, and Friday."

Owen's mouth tipped up at the corner. "And I get to walk the loop-de-loops with you the rest of the time?"

She gave a decisive nod. "Compromise. I'm told it's important in relationships."

"If I agree to this, do I get to kiss you again?"

"Probably. But you might want to wait until half the church isn't staring at us."

Owen glanced over at the crowd of open-mouthed people. Then he turned back to Kimi. "I might not care."

"I might not, either."

As soon as she uttered the words, he closed the distance between them, picked her up in a hug that left her feet dangling a good six inches off the ground.

He brushed his lips against the edge of her mouth. "I love you."

Kimi tossed the flowers to a glowing Makayla, framed Owen's face with her hands, and hoped he could see the sincerity of her heart. "I love you, too. Things won't always be easy between us. I'm going to misunderstand you sometimes, and I'm sure you'll do the same. When that happens, I don't want you to doubt my love."

"I won't. But if you ever think I've started to doubt, just do this..." His lips closed over hers again.

He pulled away, and she whispered into the charged space between them. "I'm not sure that's scientific. Don't you need a control group?"

Owen nodded. "I guess you'll have to kiss me when you don't think I'm doubting, too."

"Hm. I'm not sure that's the way it's supposed to work."

"Trust me." His words warmed her cheek. "That's exactly how it's supposed to work."

The End

Author's Note

Thank you for taking the time to read *An Informal Date*. I hope you enjoyed Owen and Kimi's story. I had a fabulous time getting to know them and unlocking the intricacies of their relationship.

If you can, please take a minute to tell others about this book by leaving a review on Amazon and Goodreads. I wouldn't mind if you told all your friends about it, too. Or took out an ad in your local paper... although that might get costly. In all seriousness, though, reviews are golden, and I appreciate every single one of them.

As a note, I did take a bit of creative license with Owen's education. It is unlikely that someone of his age would have two PhDs *and* have completed a residency.

As any writer will tell you, gratitude is a common state of being in this line of work. I am beyond thankful that God gives me stories to share and the words with which to tell them. He has allowed me to do something I love, and it's a blessing every single day. Writing isn't a solitary journey, though, and I want to thank the people who have helped pull this story together and make it shine.

Thank you E.A. West for your willingness to look over the parts of the manuscript that touched on autism to make sure I wasn't out in left field.

Thank you, also, to the ones who cheered me on while catching all my dangling modifiers and missing antecedents: Elizabeth Maddrey, Shari Shroeder, and Kay Springsteen. You're each invaluable.

About the Author

Heather loves coffee, God, her family, and laughter – not necessarily in that order! She writes approachable characters who, through the highs and lows of life, find a way to love God, embrace each day, and laugh out loud right along with her. And, yeah, her books almost always have someone who's a coffee addict. Some things just can't be helped.

She takes joy in creating characters that, much like her, are *flawed...but loved anyway.*

You can find Heather online at www.heathergraywriting.com.

Other Books by Heather Gray

Informal Romance
An Informal Christmas
An Informal Arrangement
An Informal Introduction
An Informal Date
An Informal Affair (coming spring 2017)

Ladies of Larkspur (Inspirational Western Romance)
Mail Order Man
Just Dessert
Redemption

Regency Refuge (Inspirational Regency Romance)
His Saving Grace
Jackal
Queen

Contemporary Stand-Alone Inspirational Romance
Ten Million Reasons
Nowhere for Christmas, re-releasing winter 2016

PREVIEW

An Informal Introduction
Informal Romance Book 3

Chapter One

As if the flashing lights in her rearview mirror weren't enough, the trooper turned on the siren, too. Lily cringed and slid down in her seat like a teenager hiding from prying eyes. Of course, her teen years were long behind her, and any eyes intent on prying would need night vision goggles to see her. The sun hadn't yet kissed the eastern horizon.

She slowed and sought a place to pull over, no small feat on this narrow stretch of Lee Highway. Spotting a patch of grass to her right, she steered her silver two-door sedan as far over as she could and cut the engine. Her fingers drummed a rhythmless beat on the steering wheel as she waited for the trooper. He was probably busy checking with dispatch to make sure she wasn't a mass murderer. Because, clearly, rampaging homicidal maniacs drove nondescript cars on the way to the hospital in the wee hours of the morning.

In all her years traversing this road, Lily had never seen a state trooper on this particular stretch. Until today. Good thing she'd left early for work.

Thank you, God, for getting me up and out the door when You did.

The trooper climbed out of his cruiser and approached her parked vehicle. She hit the button and listened to the almost imperceptible hum as her window slid down. The grey of his uniform would have blended into the night were it not for the illumination of his headlights and his car-mounted spotlight. As it happened, they blinded her enough that she couldn't catch much more than the color of his clothes and a hint of his shape.

"License and registration, please." The voice was impatient. Tired, too. He was probably at the end of his shift, which meant she had little chance of winning the argument, but she wouldn't let that stop her from trying.

"I wasn't speeding."

"License and registration, please."

So much for the *serve* part of public service.

"Can you at least tell me why you pulled me over?"

"Give me your license and registration, ma'am."

Heat swept through Lily. It's not like she'd asked a difficult question. "How do I even know you're a state trooper and not some crazed rapist who's trying to get my address so he can break into my home?"

The trooper's shadowed mouth hinted at a smile, and his eyes morphed from intense pinpoints to... Hm. Eyes couldn't be huggable, could they?

Who was she kidding? She couldn't even see his eyes. Her imagination had to be on overdrive.

"Well, ma'am, most people consider those flashing red and blue lights as proof enough that I'm one of the good guys, but if it would make you feel better, I'd be happy to go turn the siren back on, too. I doubt crazed rapists announce themselves with police sirens." Now that he was speaking in actual sentences, Lily picked up a hint of honeyed Southern drawl dancing along the edge of his words. She never could resist Southern charm — real or imagined.

"Here." She handed him her driver's license and the other paperwork from her glove compartment.

He examined both and called her license information in, using the small radio strapped to his left shoulder.

"For the record, I did nothing wrong."

He stepped back from her car and listened carefully to whoever was on the other end of the radio. If it was even a real person. The garbled, static-like squawking left that in doubt.

Once the radio quieted, the trooper began entering information into a form held in place on his clipboard.

Fantastic. It was never good when they started writing. Not that she had enough experience to know...

The trooper finished what he was doing and approached her window. "I'm afraid you were driving recklessly, ma'am, swerving all over the road. You're going to step out of the car and do a field sobriety test for me."

"You're kidding, right?"

The light cast by his cruiser illuminated half his face. It was enough for her to catch the widening of his eyes at her response, but it did so with a blinding glare, preventing her from making out the details of his features. "No, ma'am, I'm not joking. Please exit the car and keep your hands where I can see them."

Lily opened her door and, keeping both hands in plain sight, climbed out. "How long have you lived around here?"

The trooper ignored her question. He indicated the barely-there white stripe on the edge of the road. "I need you to walk straight down this line from your car to mine." He remained between her and the cruiser but off to the side, presumably so he wouldn't block the onboard camera filming the entire incident.

Great. She only hoped she didn't become part of some viral video about drunken nurses. True or not, it could cost her the job she loved.

She walked the line with nary a wobble. The trooper made notations on his clipboard and gave her more commands. "Touch your nose with your left index finger."

She completed each of the tasks assigned her until, at last, he produced the electronic contraption from his car. "Take a deep breath and blow into this piece here."

He indicated the straw-like attachment he'd just put on. At least she got a clean one. That was something.

With a shudder, Lily shook the thought away and did as he'd instructed.

The trooper frowned at her. "You're not drunk."

"Of course not. I was swerving to avoid all the badly-patched potholes. This road is torture on every vehicle that's ever driven it, except for the snow plows which are responsible for most of the potholes to begin with." She was only getting started. "Then spring comes, and all the holes are fixed, but this year they must have used someone new because there's not a level patch anywhere in sight. There's not a suspension system out there that can compensate for this road."

"You know the potholes and bumps so well that you can swerve around them?"

He remained cast in shadow by their position, his back to the cruiser and its too-bright lights while she stood in front of him with the glare directly in her eyes. Lily was close enough now to make out some of the geography of his face — like his square jaw — but she still couldn't identify much beyond that. Certainly not enough to tell if she was being mocked or admired. "I drive the road on my way to work. It's faster than the freeway, which is always bogged down by now. And I never once swerved out of my lane. How is it any different than if I'd been trying to avoid debris? I wasn't being unsafe. I was swerving specifically so I *could* drive safely."

The trooper scratched his head, and Lily took a moment to admire his plentiful — if short — hair. The color remained indistinguishable, but at least he wasn't bald.

Not that bald was always bad. On some men, though, it was… unfortunate.

He shook his head and moved closer to show her the clipboard. "I'm giving you a warning. As far-fetched as it sounds, your excuse might just be legit. I need you to sign and date here."

Excuse? Lily tried not to growl as she grabbed the pen from him and completed her part of the form. "Any chance you'll hang back for a while?" Like, give her a ten-minute head start before making his way from the shoulder back onto the highway? Now that she was running late for work — thanks to him — she'd have to push the speed limit.

"In a hurry?"

She shrugged and withheld the glare she wanted to give him as she reached a hand out for her copy of the warning. "I wasn't before, but I am now."

"Wherever you're in a rush to go, I'm sure it's not life or death. Drive safe and follow the laws of the road. Including the speed limit."

Lily held back the mock salute she wanted to offer him. He'd gotten her morning off to a doozy of a start, but she'd do her best not to take it out on him. She could empathize, after all. Her job was to help people, too, and it sometimes required her to call people out on their behavior or habits. It wasn't fun to be cast in the role of *bad guy* in order to do good for people.

With a glance at the road, Lily buckled her belt. In the time they'd been on the shoulder, the highway had turned from a ghost town into a quagmire of early morning traffic. Making it to work on time was out of the question now. With a disgruntled mutter, she tucked the earpiece into place and hit a button on her steering wheel. "Call ICU." It was time to tell the charge nurse she would be late.

"Pulled over for drunk driving?"

Lily hung her head as she scrubbed in at the sink.

"Child, you have the kind of luck that gives most folks hound dog jowls." Lyza, the nurse she was scheduled to replace, leaned against the wall next to her and waited.

Could anyone talk to Lyza and not smile? "I don't own a hound dog, and hopefully I never develop jowls, but I appreciate the sentiment. I was supposed to get here early, too. Sorry they made you stay late for me."

With the lift of a shoulder, Lyza dismissed it. "No worries. I'm off the next three nights, and the extra thirty minutes was worth it to hear your story." The older nurse chuckled again. "Drunk driving. Unbelievable."

Lily would face a day full of good-natured ribbing about her escapades with a state trooper, but she didn't mind. Life in ICU could be wrapped up with a single word: intense. Being the occasional butt of a joke only meant people had something to laugh about. Tomorrow it would be somebody else's turn to lighten the mood with their own embarrassing story.

Lyza gave her the rundown. "Mr. Miller is your only patient for now. My other one got moved out to the floor two hours ago. Since you were late, they shuffled the assignments."

"If anybody else comes in today, they're all mine." Lily knew the drill. In all likelihood, she'd be in charge of another patient by lunchtime. ICU was rarely dull, Mondays especially so. Her *drunk driving* experience was sure to be only the start of an adventuresome day. "All right, then. Tell me about Mr. Miller."

"He works at one of the tire recycling places around here. The tires go through a shredder there before they can go on to the next phase of processing. Only something got jammed, and he shut the machine down to search for the problem, but some trainee who'd been out back smoking a cigarette with earbuds blasting who-knows-what into his ears and drowning out the PA announcement came along and blew it all to smithereens by pushing the big red button that started the shredder back up."

"Oh, no." Lily's stomach dropped.

Lyza took a big breath and exhaled, fluffing her bangs as she did so. "Fool kid could've killed someone, but luckily the supervisor shut the machine back off within seconds. Mr. Miller's arm was decimated. He was in the OR for hours but the doctors couldn't save it. There are a lot of other contusions and bruises, but the amputation is the worst. He ended up with an SD."

Shoulder disarticulation. His arm had been removed at the shoulder joint. As often happened with patients brought into the ICU, his life was headed in a whole new direction.

Lord, help him adapt.

Lily was helping Jacie, one of the newer nurses, with a bedding change in room 4150 when the charge nurse — whose voice carried across the unit even if she whispered — yelled from the front desk. "Lily, we got a hot one coming in! Now!"

She spared a quick "Gotta run" for Jacie before peeling off her gloves and leaving Mrs. Rivera's room behind her.

"Tell me what we know." How much information they received depended greatly on where a patient came from. Sometimes the details were sketchy at best.

The charge nurse, with her short gun-metal grey hair and perpetual frown, was all business. "Female, fifty-five years old. Son found her collapsed and phoned for an ambulance. ER cites severe dehydration and ketoacidosis. She's ours until we can get her blood sugar stable."

Lily nodded. "You said hot?" That was a term they used when a patient was combative.

"Not her. The son. All they told me is that most of the emergency room emptied out as soon as he marched in."

Oh, dear. Gang banger? Giant Samoan wrestler? Covered in body art and piercings? Please don't let him have metal spikes drilled into his skull like that guy last month!

Lily took the paperwork from the charge nurse. She peeked in on Mr. Miller — no change there — before moving on to open the glass doors of Mrs. — she glanced at the papers — Graham's room for the transport team to wheel her hospital bed into place.

"Hi, Mrs. Graham. My name's Lily, and I'm going to be your nurse today. Are you comfortable? Can I get you anything?"

"No, dear, I'm fine. Everybody's making way too much fuss. I'd rather be allowed to go home."

A visual assessment of the patient showed bright eyes and good color. Her speech was clear, too. Lily made a couple notes on the chart then tugged the stethoscope from around her neck and placed its diaphragm against her hand to warm it. "I need to listen to your heart and lungs for a second. This might be cold. Try to ignore me and breathe like normal."

The rustle of movement behind her announced someone's entry, most likely the son.

"Caleb, dear, will you please say hello to Lily? She's my nurse."

She gritted her teeth behind a bright smile as she circled to greet Mrs. Graham's son, the man who had single-handedly driven everyone out of the Emergency Room. Lily ended up face-to-face with a whole lot of grey. The man wore a uniform, and not just any uniform. A quick step back allowed her to look up at his face without having to crane her neck.

Her gaze raked across his unshaven jawline and grey eyes, but that wasn't where her attention landed. A well-worn cowboy hat topped his head in place of the typical state trooper's campaign hat.

A uniform and a cowboy hat both... Good thing she wasn't the type to get weak in the knees.

"Hey, Lily." Rinaldo, one of the respiratory techs, hollered to her as he approached the door. "Police are on the unit. Did they come to haul you away after your run-in this morning?" The tech popped his head over the threshold, but as he took in the scene, his eyes grew into saucers and he backpedaled out the door. Lily watched from the corner of her eye as her friend abandoned her and sped down the corridor.

"I hope you nurse in a straighter line than you drive."

That voice!

She hadn't gotten a good look at the trooper. During her sobriety test, he'd stayed between her and the cruiser, backlit the entire time. She'd been in the spotlight while he'd remained in the shadows. He would have had a clear view of her, but she'd not been able to garner much more than an impression of his appearance. His voice, though, pure velvet with the subtle hint of a Southern drawl, was unforgettable.

"You!"

Made in the USA
Middletown, DE
24 January 2023

22684923R00111